MW00581432

Also by Sherry A. Burton
That Feeling
Tears of Betrayal
Somewhere In My Dreams
The King of My Heart
Surviving the Storm
Seems Like Yesterday
"Whispers of the Past," a short story.

Love in the Bluegrass
Sequel to Tears of Betrayal

Written by Sherry A. Burton

Love in the Bluegrass © Copyright 2018
by Sherry A. Burton
ISBN: 978-0-9983796-1-6

Published by Dorry Press
Photo by Nicole Garman,
www.garmanphotography.com
Edited and Formatted by BZHercules.com
Cover by Laura J. Prevost
@laurajprevostphotography

All rights reserved. No part of this book may be reproduced in any form or by any electronic or mechanical means, including information storage and retrieval systems—except in the case of brief quotations embodied in critical articles or reviews—without permission in writing from the author at Sherry@sherryaburton.com This book is a work of fiction. The characters, events, and places portrayed in this book are products of the author's imagination and are either fictitious or are used fictitiously. Any similarity to real persons, living or dead, is purely coincidental and not intended by the author.

For more information on the author and her works, please see www.SherryABurton.com

Acknowledgements

To my husband, Don, the calming voice in a not-so-calm world. You truly are my Prince Charming. May the fairytale continue…

To my friend, cover artist, and graphic designer, Laura Prevost, thanks for all you do to keep me current.

To my editor Beth, thanks for cutting through the weeds.

To my eagle-eyed beta and proof readers, Becky, Deb, Lisa, Laura, Tina, Tracie, Trish H., Trish Mc., Ruth, and Sandy, thanks for being on my team!

To my fans, thank you for the continued support.

Lastly, to my voices, thank you for choosing me.

Dedication

To my late Aunt Dianna, the Wildcats were added just for you.

Table of Contents

Chapter One

Amber stared at the plastic wand in her hand, mentally willing the lines to turn pink. She sighed, knowing the effort fruitless. It was well past the allotted time – no amount of wishing would reverse the results. As much as she wanted to have a child with Dalton, it was most likely not going to happen. They'd tried everything the fertility doctor suggested: taking her temperature, fertility drugs, and even abstaining, something that was extremely difficult for both. After several days of abstinence, they'd finally given up that part, deciding to let fate lead their way. According to the doctors, the problem lay with Dalton – a low sperm count. She smiled, remembering their latest encounter. How could someone as amorous as Dalton Renfro have a low sperm count? Her smile widened. One thing was certain: if she did not get pregnant, it was not from lack of trying. It had been that way since she'd wed Dalton just over four years ago.

She sighed, remembering the simple ceremony. Nothing fancy, just the two of them surrounded by a handful of family and a few very close friends. She felt her heart flutter. Four wonderful years, during which time she had finally come to life. Before meeting and falling in love with

Dalton, she had merely been alive. A living and breathing shell. Closing her eyes, she took in a deep breath and gave thanks for the many blessings in her life.

Goosebumps rose the length of her arms as she recalled the fateful horoscope that had predicted the death of her then-husband, Jeff. *Tragedy is a blessing in disguise*, it had read. The message had proven true in so many ways. After his death, she'd found out her husband had cheated on her throughout her marriage, and that his current girlfriend was pregnant with his child. Guilt replaced the goosebumps as she thought of the child and the secret she now kept. She pictured the boy who looked very much like the man who had fathered him. Anger flashed as her thoughts turned to her late husband and how he'd deceived her until the very end. She'd received divorce papers on the day of his funeral. Over four years and her anger remained palpable. Anger at Jeff. Anger at herself for being so damn gullible. She'd been the dutiful wife. He'd taken everything she had to give. He nearly sucked the life right out of her, and she was so busy trying to please him that she'd not even noticed. He would have succeeded too, had he not been killed before he was able to follow through with his plan, the one intended to leave her blindsided and destitute. Lucky for her, fate had intervened, severing their marriage, only not in the way her husband had planned. Amber took one last longing look at the wand before giving up and setting it on the nightstand.

Moving to the window, she drew open the heavy drapes, allowing the morning sun to wash over her. She loved that their bedroom caught the morning sun. Closing her eyes, she bathed in the brilliant sunlight, letting it warm her body. She'd peered out the window every morning since her arrival, never once tiring of the view, always feeling as if she'd finally come home. She felt safe nestled within the white fencing that stretched for miles, encompassing the hundreds of acres of the estate known as Sunset Meadows. This morning, a blanket of freshly fallen snow covered pastures, a stark contrast to the black fencing nearer the house and barns. Several horses had the run of the field closer to the main house. She watched as the horses, covered with warming blankets, frolicked in the field, high-stepping in the late season snow. She pressed her forehead against the cool windowpane and let out a contented sigh.

A light rap at the door drew her attention.

"Come in," she said, turning from the window.

The large woman entered, her gaze darting despairingly over the freshly made bed. "Child, I sure do wish you would let me do my job."

Amber held her tongue. It was not the first time they'd had this conversation. Maggie was the glue that held the house together after Dalton's first wife, Mary Katherine, had passed shortly after the birth of their daughter, Katie Mae. The elderly lady was the only mother figure the child had known until Amber came into the picture. Amber smiled at the woman. Having lost her own mother when she was young, Amber welcomed Maggie's mothering ways. In some aspects, she felt as if she'd gained both a husband and a mother at the same time. Maggie cooked, cleaned, worried over the family, and never failed to give her opinion on the situation at hand. While she was paid very well for her services, she was as much a member of the family as Amber herself.

"Maggie, we've been through this. You have enough to do. I am perfectly capable of making my bed. It's bad enough you won't let me help with the laundry."

"Hmph," Maggie opened her mouth to reply, but her gaze landed on the plastic wand on the nightstand. Her glance shifted to Amber. "Anything I should know?"

Amber shook her head. "No... still nothing."

"Land sakes, child. It breaks my heart that two people who love each other can't bring a baby into the world."

Amber closed her eyes briefly before answering.

"Maggie, I know it's crazy to want another child so much. Especially since we have Julie and Katie Mae, but I would love to give Dalton a son. I had given up all hope of having another baby when I was married to Jeff. After Julie was born, Jeff was adamant about not having any more children."

Her stomach clenched. She knew now that it was not that her late husband didn't want another child; he did not want the child he'd had with her. He'd fathered a son that had been born several months after his death. She was almost grateful that Jeff had died. It would have broken her heart knowing he was doting on a son when he'd never given their daughter more than a few minutes of his time. A chill traveled up her arms as she thought of his other child – pudgy-faced, sandy blonde hair and green eyes – a miniature replica of his father. She pushed the child from her thoughts.

Maggie narrowed her eyes. "Miss Julie is better off with the daddy she has now."

Amber smiled in acknowledgement. Julie had begun calling Dalton "Dad" shortly after they had said their vows. In the short time they'd been married, Julie had spent more time with Dalton than she had with her own father in the first thirteen and a half years of her life.

"There is no doubt in my mind about that, Maggie. Dalton has treated her like his own from the first time he helped her onto a horse. That's the point, he is so good with children, and I know he would like to have more. I just wish we could get pregnant."

Maggie wrung her hands. "Well, if it is meant to be, it will be. But it is not going to happen with you staying up here fretting about it. Sometimes it is best just to relax and let nature take its course. I once knew a woman who wanted a baby. She and her husband kept trying and trying but never could get pregnant. As soon as they decided it was not going to happen, they ended up with twins. You said it before, Miss Amber. Between the two of you, you've got some mighty fine young'uns. If the Lord wants you to have another, he will make sure a child comes your way."

Amber smiled at the woman who always seemed to have an answer for everything. "Maggie, how'd you get to be so wise?"

The large lady snorted in response. "Ain't nothing to it. When you have been around as long as I have, you just know things to be true."

Before Amber could respond, a shrill voice pierced the air. "Momma! Miss Maggie! Breakfast is ready!"

Amber moved to the nightstand and grasped the small wand, tucking it into her pocket just as Katie bolted into the room. Clancy bounded in only seconds behind, his nubby tail twitching from side to side at a frantic pace. Amber reached down and hugged the child, kissing her softly on her dimpled cheek. Clancy took the opportunity to give Amber a wet kiss of his own, his tongue slobbering eagerly across an exposed ear. "Ugh! Dog breath! Knock it off, you crazy mutt."

Pushing the dog away, she stood and appraised the girl who was staring back at her, a nearly toothless smile plastered on her face. Her black shoulder-length hair was neatly combed and held back at the sides with blue Kentucky Wildcat barrettes. She was wearing jeans and a U of K sweatshirt with a blue wildcat that matched her barrettes along with the laces in her sneakers. At eight years old, the little girl was the epitome of a University of Kentucky fan. Amber smiled at her step-daughter, who she loved as dearly as her own. It melted her heart each time the girl called her Mom, something she had never insisted on. At first, Katie called her Amber Mae, then after hearing Julie and Kelly, her new niece, call her Mom, Katie had taken to calling her Momma Amber, then in a natural osmosis, she simply called her Momma or Mom.

Amber reached out, adjusting one of the girl's barrettes. "I see you are ready to go to the game with Mamal and Papal. Are you excited?"

Maggie let out a snort of laughter, and Katie looked at Amber as if she'd suddenly taken leave of her senses. Amber rolled her eyes upwards as if asking forgiveness. Of course the little girl was excited. She loved the Wildcats. Heck, nearly everyone who lived in the town counted them as their favorite team. Even Amber, not normally a basketball fan, could not help getting caught up in all the hoopla. After moving to Lexington, it was little surprise that her oldest daughter, Julie, had also succumbed to Wildcat fever. Still, while Julie had crossed over to Kentucky in basketball, nothing could break her bond and love for the Detroit Red Wings hockey team.

Realizing she had just made a grave mom mistake, Amber hurried to change the subject. "Is Julie ready too? Your grandparents are supposed to pick you up right after breakfast."

As if on cue, the lanky teen rounded the corner. Julie had inherited her height from her mother. At seventeen, Julie matched Amber's five-foot-seven. Her long brown hair had been pulled back into its signature ponytail and tied with blue and white ribbons. She was wearing a white Kentucky Wildcat sweatshirt, a brave move, given the fact that her face sported bright blue paint. "Miss Barbara said to tell you breakfast is ready."

Seeing Julie's face, Katie's eyes lit up with awe. "I want a blue face too."

Julie turned to her sister. "Breakfast is ready. We won't have time to paint your whole face, but I can paint something on your cheek before we leave if we hurry."

Appeased, the younger child turned to Amber. "Hurry, Mom. Hurry, Miss Maggie. We have to go eat so I have time to get my face painted," she pleaded before grabbing her sister's hand and leaving the room.

Following the girls out of the room, Amber hesitated at the door. She'd spent the morning concentrating on things she could not control. After spending years in an unhappy marriage, she now had everything she'd ever wished for: a husband who adored her and two daughters that made her heart swell with pride. Turning to Maggie, she smiled.

"How did I ever get so lucky, Maggie?"

Maggie patted her arm. "I have always heard it said, when you give thanks for what you have, you open yourself up to receive more."

Suddenly, guilt gnawed at Amber. "It's time for me to stop being selfish. I have so many wonderful people in my life. I will start focusing more on them and not on the what ifs."

"It's not a sin to want more, child. You have so much love to share. Just make sure you don't lose sight of what you already have when you are seeking the rest."

Amber placed her hand on top of Maggie's and heaved a sigh. "How about we go join the rest of our family for breakfast."

Chapter Two

The aroma of bacon greeted them as they entered the dining room. A platter piled high with salty strips sat in the middle of the table, beckoning all who entered to delight their taste buds with the crispy fare. A bowl of fluffy yellow eggs sat next to it; beside that, a plate of thinly sliced yellow tomatoes. A glass pitcher of milk, another containing orange juice, and a stainless steel coffee carafe sat at the end of the table.

Amber watched as Maggie surveyed the table with a critical eye before smiling her approval at the tall, slender woman, who had just entered the room with a heaping plate of buttermilk pancakes and a small ceramic container of warm maple syrup. The woman was in her late sixties and quite becoming. Naturally frosted silver locks sprang out in short soft curls, a look that would have cost a fortune to duplicate in a salon. Her rough age-spotted hands were the only real sign of her advanced age.

"You girls may as well go on and start. At least you've both got the good graces to be at the breakfast table on time," the woman said, placing the plate of pancakes within reach of Julie and Katie.

"Thanks, Miss Barbara," both girls chimed jointly, reaching for their forks and filling their plates in compatible silence.

Barbara patted her forehead with the edge of her apron and brushed at a wayward curl. "I don't want the young'uns to be running off without a full belly," she said by way of explanation.

"Now if I can rein in the menfolk, the rest of us just may be able to enjoy a hot breakfast as well. Men! I swear you tell them precisely when to be here, and they still can't make it on time. It's not as if I go and change up the time on a daily basis. No, we have our meals at the same time every single day. But do you see them?"

Maggie lowered herself onto her chair. "Land sakes, Barbara, you sound like an old goose with all your squawking. The men have been out in the barn all night. I heard a racket near round three in the morn. Came into the kitchen to see what was amiss and found Dalton rootin around the pantry, looking for some coffee. Said one of the mares was foaling early. I made him a carafe to take out to the others and ain't seen hide nor hair of any of 'em since."

Amber suppressed a giggle. Though the two looked nothing alike, the women seemed to mirror each other in their speech. She let out a long, contented sigh, grateful that the two ladies were getting along so well. Amber had repeatedly offered to help with the housework, but Maggie would have no part of it. The woman was old school, and in her mind, it was not right for the Lady of the Manor to do the housework, especially when Maggie was paid to do the job. The quandary was, as the family expanded, so did the woman's workload. The added work, extreme stubbornness, and Maggie's immense size took its toll on the elderly woman, who ended up in the emergency room. After being diagnosed with both high blood pressure and diabetes, Maggie started on insulin and hypertension drugs. It was also highly recommended she lower her stress level and lose weight. After her release, Dalton had put his foot down, telling Maggie the only way she could come home was if she promised to hire someone to help ease her workload. As much as Maggie had hated to admit it, she knew she could no longer do everything on her own. Since she had to be on a strict diet, it was decided she should find someone to take over the kitchen duties and meal preparation to help keep her from temptation. That created yet another problem, as Maggie could not seem to find anyone she deemed competent enough to help. The problem solved itself a short time later when Maggie's cousin, Barbara, lost her job. Barbara herself had worked as a live-in house caretaker for years, until the gentleman she'd been caring for passed away, leaving her not only jobless but homeless as well. Barbara moved in, eased the workload on Maggie, and had become an instant member of the ever-expanding household. Sunset Meadows, the name Dalton had given his expansive estate, was running smoothly, and everyone appeared happy with the new arrangement.

Maggie cast a despairing glance at the row of empty seats. The look wasn't lost on Barbara, who pulled out her cell phone and placed a call as she left the room.

Amber smiled. While it should be her place to call her husband to the breakfast table, she preferred to let Maggie and Barbara do the mothering, something they both seemed born to do, even though neither woman had children of her own. Amber felt another pang of guilt for her selfishness. She had two daughters – one biological, one not of her blood – both of whom she loved equally.

Barbara returned, carrying a bowl piled high with golden biscuits. "Dalton and Travis will be right in. They were just leaving the barn when I called. Carl and Jake are staying with the mare."

Amber heard the door open and took her seat at the table across from the girls. She didn't miss the look of disappointment that passed over Julie's face at the mention of Jake, the ranch's youngest hired hand. Plainly, Julie was suffering from a major schoolgirl crush. At least she hoped that was all it was. She made a mental note to ask Julie about it later.

Dalton entered the room, drawing her attention away from Julie. His gaze met hers, the corners of his eyes crinkling when he saw her. She felt her heart flutter. It had been that way since the first moment she'd seen him, just over four years ago at the fairgrounds. He looked pretty much the same now as he had then: handsomely disheveled, a low-slung black cowboy hat hovering over bloodshot eyes, tired from lack of sleep. He'd driven all night to surprise his niece, Kelly, for her birthday. Kelly turned out to be Julie's best friend. Introductions were made, and the rest was, as they say, history. A whirlwind courtship ended with a trip to the justice of the peace.

Dalton's eyes remained on hers as he removed his hat and placed it on a hook along the back wall of the dining room. She drank in the sight of him, knowing that no matter how much time they had together, it would never be enough. He had a way of looking at her as if she were the only one in the room. The heat of his stare suddenly made her wish that were the case. His hair was tousled and he sported a dark five o'clock shadow, lending to his appeal. She smiled. *How is it that he can be up for hours and still look as if he just stepped off the cover of cowboy calendar?*

He winked at her, bent to kiss Julie on the cheek, and froze. He pulled back, kissing her on top of her head instead. He repeated the process with Katie before rounding the table and giving Amber a lingering kiss.

Julie and Katie snickered.

Ending the kiss, Dalton took his place at the end of the table. "Interesting paint job there, Julie," he said, placing his napkin in his lap.

"It's for the game, Dad," Katie offered. "She's going to paint mine after breakfast if we have time."

"Where's Grandpa?" Julie asked before shoving a fork full of pancake into her mouth.

"I'm right here."

All heads turned as Amber's father, Travis, entered the room. Dark circles tugged at his swollen eyes; his thin cheeks carried a heavy growth of grey. His hand trembled as he pulled back the chair and took a seat next to Julie. Travis had moved in with them shortly after the wedding. He had a longstanding relationship with alcohol, which caused a strained one with Amber, who had balked when Dalton first suggested her father move in with them. Dalton, who believed in family, insisted the power of love and family support could be a strong tool in overcoming life's obstacles. So far, this seemed to be the case. Travis had slipped a couple of times, but lately, with the help of Alcoholics Anonymous, seemed to be keeping the beast at bay. Amber opened her mouth to question his appearance but fell silent when Dalton placed his hand on top of hers.

"Travis has been out in the barn all night. One of the mares is ready to drop her foal. She's early, so Jake and Carl are staying with her. They promised to call when she gets close." He gave her a gentle caress before releasing her hand.

"I hope you had the good sense to wash up before you came in here." Maggie was not as convinced of Travis' sobriety and watched him like a hawk.

"We both did," Dalton said, jumping to the man's defense. He scooped out a heaping helping of fried potatoes before passing the bowl to Amber. That set the wheels in motion for others to load their plates with what was in front of them before, in turn, passing the dish to the next person. Amber relished the large meals that were commonplace on the ranch. Having been left mostly to her own devices after her mom died, she rarely ate a real meal as a family until after she and Dalton were married. Even in her previous marriage to Jeff, except holidays, meals were eaten in front of the television and talking was kept to a minimum, lest they interrupt the program.

Dalton was old school, in that meals were to be enjoyed as a family, when possible, and always in the dining room.

Barbara passed the biscuit bowl to Travis and smiled. "Come into the kitchen after breakfast, and I will pack you some food to take to Jake and Carl."

Travis mumbled his thanks, took a biscuit, and passed the bowl to Maggie.

The breakfast table was alive with easy chatter and clanking silverware. Amber took a bite of eggs and watched as the girls hurried through their breakfast, each rushing to have time to finish getting ready for the big game. Normally, she would have fussed at them to slow down but knew her advice would not be heeded for long. Instead, she smiled, knowing how she would have felt in their place. Dalton, always the voice of reason, had told her she needed to pick her battles where the girls were concerned. The advice made sense and staved off plenty of arguments when it came to a battle of wills.

"Any idea when the foal will drop?" Maggie asked.

"It shouldn't be too long now," Dalton said.

Amber watched Maggie's nostrils flare as Dalton took two strips of bacon from the platter. The woman sighed and dipped her spoon into her bowl of oatmeal.

"More bacon?" Dalton asked, passing the plate to Amber.

"No, I'll pass," Amber said, not having the heart to torture the woman further. She heard a sigh and smiled as Maggie dipped her spoon into the bowl of oatmeal sitting in front of her. While still extremely large, the woman had made great strides in her weight loss.

"How about you, Travis?" Barbara said, smiling warmly at the man. "A full belly keeps what ails you at bay."

"It's going to take a lot more than bacon today," Travis said, nodding his head.

"Such as?" Amber said coldly.

Travis looked at her over the rim of his coffee cup. "Caffeine, honey. A day like this calls for caffeine and lots of it."

Amber felt her face flush. Of course he wanted coffee. He'd been up half the night. She realized that his appearance was not much different than that of Dalton and silently chastised herself for being so hard on the man. She just couldn't help herself. A part of her was still angry at him for reaching for the bottle after her mom had died, instead of stepping up to the plate and being a father. She had been lonely as a child and even lonelier as an adult, becoming pregnant while still in high school and marrying a man who was never home.

"Mom?" Julie asked, pulling her back to the present.

"What?"

"I asked if I could be excused," Julie said.

"Yes, of course," Amber said, embarrassed that she didn't hear the question the first time.

"Me too?" Katie asked hopefully.

"You too," Amber said, smiling. "Try not to make a mess with the paint," she said as both girls hurried from the room.

"I think I'll go and check on the mare's progress," Travis said, pushing his plate away.

"I'll be out shortly," Dalton said, pouring more coffee into his cup.

"If the offer still stands, I'm sure the guys could do with some grub," Travis said to Barbara, who jumped up and hurried to the kitchen. Travis followed on her heels, looking much like a love-struck puppy.

Maggie lowered her spoon into her now empty bowl with a clang. "Land sakes, seems like everyone is in a rush this morning."

She hefted herself from the chair, gathered several plates, and disappeared into the kitchen.

"You seem a bit preoccupied this morning," Dalton said once they were alone.

"Just having an off day is all," Amber said. *That is putting it mildly.*

Dalton brought her hand to his mouth, kissing the ring on her left hand. "Anything I can do?"

"Why are you so good to me?" she asked, relishing his touch.

"It's my job," he said warmly.

"You do it so well." She sighed. *What is wrong with me? I have everything I need and then some.*

Dalton's phone buzzed. He reached for it, frowning at the screen. "Looks like things are happening in the barn."

"Go, I'll see you later."

He gave her a quick kiss, scooped up his hat, and hurried from the room, his attention already on the happenings in the barn.

Travis burst through the door carrying several sacks. "Gotta go, gotta go. There's a baby coming into the world," he said, following Dalton's path.

A baby coming into the world, Amber repeated silently. Her thoughts drifted to the letter she'd received in the mail two days prior, the one offering to give her everything she felt was missing, the letter that had left her feeling as if she were surrounded by ghosts.

Chapter Three

Amber stared out the window, watching as several cars came to a stop at the traffic light on Broadway. Impatiently, she sipped her coffee, wishing her friend would hurry. Robin, her best friend of twelve plus years, was ten minutes past due, and it wasn't like her to be late. Amber had tried texting, but so far had not received a reply – another rarity, as Robin was always quick to respond. The door opened. Amber sighed as a woman made her way into the building, stomping the snow from her high boots. Amber watched as the lady acknowledged another woman, then hurried to get in line. Amber looked out the window once more, wondering what was keeping her friend.

Robin was Amber's confidante, a true friend who had been there every step of the way since their first unlikely meeting. Amber's thoughts went to when they had met all those years ago at the grocery store. Julie, who was only three at the time, pulled a container of flour off a shelf, dousing Robin with flour. Most people would have freaked out, but not Robin; it had been the beginning of a solid friendship. Amber wondered how solid that friendship would be after she told Robin why she'd invited her here.

The door opened. Relief washed over Amber as Robin entered. Robin pushed her blonde hair out of her flushed face, which lit up upon seeing Amber. She held up a finger, placed her order, and then joined Amber at her table.

"It's crazy out there. It took forever to find a parking spot," Robin said, hugging Amber.

"Sorry, I guess I should have picked someplace with an actual parking lot. I tried to text you; I was getting worried."

Robin pulled her phone out of her pocket. "Dang phone doesn't have a signal here. Now that we've moved here, we are going to be changing providers."

"How are you liking the new house?"

"I'll like it more when I have everything put where it belongs. The house is a total wreck right now," Robin said, taking a drink of her coffee.

"I offered to come up and help you unpack," Amber reminded her.

"I know, but you know me; I prefer to do it all myself. That way, I know where everything is."

"Spoken like a true control freak," Amber teased.

"Like a true Navy wife, is more like it," Robin said.

"Who is also a control freak," Amber said.

"Yeah, there's that too." Robin laughed.

"I'm just glad you and Jack decided to move closer."

"Well, with you and Lana both gone, Michigan just didn't feel like home anymore. Jack is always away with the Navy, and my parents aren't getting any younger, so it seemed the logical choice. Now if I could only convince the kids to move to Kentucky too," Robin said with a frown. Connor, Robin's oldest son, had lived with Robin's parents in Louisville, Kentucky for a short time, but had since returned to Alliance, Michigan, where Regan, Robin's only daughter, lived. Logan, the baby of the family, had enlisted in the Marines straight out of high school and was stationed in North Carolina.

"Missing them?"

"Yeah, but at least we can Skype," Robin said, brightening. "So I get the feeling your insisting we meet was more than just needing to talk, especially since we do that every day."

Amber smiled. Robin could always read her so well. She sighed, wondering where to begin. Guilt had a way of making one feel dirty, especially when it came to neglecting a child.

Robin took another sip of her coffee, obviously waiting until Amber was ready to tell her what was on her mind.

"I'm a terrible person," Amber said at last. "I've been keeping something from you. Worse than that, I've kept it from Dalton as well."

Robin raised her eyebrows.

"This ought to be good," she said, leaning closer.

"I'm serious," Amber continued. "Do you remember Heather?"

Robin twisted her mouth in thought. "Nope, the name's not ringing a bell."

"Jeff's girlfriend. You met her at his funeral," Amber said.

"Oh, the pregnant whore. Why didn't you just say so?"

"Yeah, well, she's not pregnant anymore."

Robin laughed. "It's been four years; I would hope not. Let me guess. She's looking for more money than what you generously left the brat."

Amber smiled at her friend, always one to speak her mind. "No, that's not it."

Robin sat back. "So are you going to tell me what this is all about, or would you prefer I keep guessing?"

"How about you read it for yourself?" Amber said, pulling three envelopes from her purse. Opening the first, she handed it to Robin and listened as she read the letter out loud.

GRETHER LAW OFFICES, P.C.
SUITE 1364
MAIN STREET TOWER   TELEPHONE: (810) 555-5555
300 EAST MAIN STREET   TELEFAX: (810) 555-5551
Alliance, MI 48471
E-MAIL: bhaden@bestlex.com

Re: *A child is born*

Dear Mrs. Renfro;

As your attorney, I feel at liberty to inform you of the birth of one Matthew Daxton Wilson, the son of Ms. Heather Cummings and your late husband, Jeffery Wilson. The trust fund you initiated on the child's behalf is in place and will be officiated by my office to ensure the monies spent are for the direct care and well-being of the child.

I feel it my duty to inform you the mother is in poor health. Alas, I am not at liberty to speak as to the specific condition, only that the outcome may not be to her liking and may warrant appointing a permanent guardian for the aforementioned child. I am telling you this in the strictest of confidence as your attorney and friend. I will keep you apprised as to the situation.

V/R,
John Grether

Robin folded the paper and handed it to Amber. "So she's sick. How does that make you a bad person?"

Amber took the paper and slid it into the envelope before handing Robin a second letter, which Robin once again read aloud.

GRETHER LAW OFFICES, P.C.
SUITE 1364
MAIN STREET TOWER   TELEPHONE: (810) 555-5555
300 EAST MAIN STREET   TELEFAX: (810) 555-5551
Alliance, MI 48471
E-MAIL: bhaden@bestlex.com

Re: Matthew Daxton Wilson

Dear Mrs. Renfro,

I'm contacting you on behalf of Heather Cummings. As I'm sure you are aware, Ms. Cummings is the mother of the child, Matthew Daxton Wilson. I informed you previously that Ms. Cummings was ill. As anticipated, her health has continued to worsen to a point to where she is no longer able to care for her infant son. Ms. Cummings' parents are doing their best to care for the child. However, they are of advanced age and fear they will not be able to continue doing so much longer. I have contacted the father's family, all of which have asked to receive no future updates as to this situation.

I realize I am going out on a limb here, but since you showed such great compassion for the then unborn child at the time of your husband's passing, I thought maybe you would look kindly upon the boy, who as you know, is a sibling to your daughter, Julie.

Ms. Cummings' parents have asked me to contact you, to see if you would be interested in adopting the child, stating they have full power of attorney over their daughter who is not long for this world.

Please advise how you wish to proceed.

V/R
John Grether
Picture enclosed

Robin handed the letter to Amber, keeping her hand extended for the final letter Amber was holding.

GRETHER LAW OFFICES, P.C.
SUITE 1364

MAIN STREET TOWER   TELEPHONE: (810) 555-5555
300 EAST MAIN STREET   TELEFAX: (810) 555-5551
Alliance, MI 48471
E-MAIL: bhaden@bestlex.com

Re: <u>Matthew Daxton Wilson</u>

Dear Mrs. Renfro,

In regard to my previous letters, I am writing to ask you to reconsider your decision on the matter concerning Matthew Daxton Wilson. The mother's condition remains grave and her parents, being in poor health themselves, are no longer able to care for the aforementioned child. With no other family members willing to take the child, I am afraid he has been placed in foster care. The mother's parents have begged me once more to contact you, to see if you would consider adopting the child. The mother has also promised to sever all ties, which at this point is a mere legality given the seriousness of her condition. What this does is award custody directly to you, to help navigate the legal channels much more smoothly. The mother, during her moments of lucidity, is adamant that no member of the father's family be given custody, not that any have shown any interest in the child during the past three and a half years. I am aware of your previous decision to keep your distance but implore you to reconsider and take this innocent child into your care.

Very respectfully yours,

John Grether

P.S. I have taken the liberty of enclosing a recent photo of the child.

Robin peered over the letter she had just finished reading, moisture dampening her eyes.

"So is there a reason you chose not to share this bit of news with me?" she asked, the hurt evident in her voice.

"For the same reason your expression says. You think I should adopt the child."

"And you don't?" Robin asked.

"How can I?"

"What do you mean?" Robin asked. "How long have you been trying to get pregnant? And this innocent little boy is being raised by the system, just because his poor mother can't care for him."

Amber took the letter, folded it, and stuffed it back into the envelope. "A few minutes ago, the mother was a whore and the child a brat."

"That was before I found out the woman was dying. Hand it over," she said, draining her cup.

"Hand what over?" Amber asked.

"I'm not in the mood to play. Just let me see the damn picture," Robin said, holding her hand out and snapping her fingers.

Amber pulled out the most recent picture and handed it to Robin, whose face softened upon seeing it. Amber knew what her friend was seeing: bright green eyes staring out of a cherub face beneath a mop of sandy blonde hair. A face that would melt the heart of anyone who looked at it, hers included, if he did not look so very much like his father. How could she even consider adopting a child that would be a daily reminder of her late husband's infidelity? Hadn't she been through enough? Didn't she deserve some happiness? Unfortunately, deserving to be happy and being happy were two different things, as she had not had a clear conscience since receiving the second letter over a year ago, the one that pulled at her heart, and made her dream of green-eyed babies.

Amber studied Robin's face, trying to gauge her thoughts. Mostly what she saw was disappointment.

"I've never known you to be at a loss for words," Amber said at last.

"I'm just trying to figure out what I want to say first," Robin replied.

"Just say what's on your mind. I doubt anything you can say is any worse than anything I've already said to myself at least a hundred times."

"First, let me say that I'm disappointed," Robin said, confirming Amber's deductions. "We are friends, best friends, or at least I thought so."

"Of course we are," Amber said.

"Yes, and with very few exceptions, we talk every day, and yet this is the first I've heard about the child."

"I know, I'm sorry."

"It's not just me, Amber. You've been married to the man of your dreams for four years, and correct me if I'm wrong, but you haven't shared any of this with him either."

"No..."

"You once sat in your kitchen crying, telling me you wanted what I had – a wonderful relationship, a soul mate with whom you could share everything. Until now I thought you had found that."

"I have. Dalton is amazing. He's everything I've ever wanted and then some," Amber countered.

"Well, he has to be lacking somewhere, or you would feel confident enough to tell him about the child. What, are you afraid he will say no?" Robin asked.

"On the contrary, I'm afraid he will say yes," Amber said.

Robin leaned forward and lowered her voice. "Did that asshole ex-husband of yours F you up that much? Did he harden your heart so much that you cannot see your way to help a child that is being handed to you on a silver platter? Do you know how long regular adoptions take? Years! Do you know how long it takes a child to get lost in the system? If he's lucky, he will find a family to adopt him. If not, he will probably suffer from years of moving from family to family, all while you are sitting in your big house, pining away for the child you never had."

"It's not the same. Look at the picture, Robin. He looks just like his father. Every time I see him, I will see Jeff. What if I can't handle that? What if I punish the child for the sins of his father?"

Robin looked her straight in the eye. "Girlfriend, if you ask me, you already are."

Both women sat there in silence, each thinking their thoughts until finally, Robin broke the silence.

"Why did you ask me to come?"

"What do you mean?"

"You could have told me all of this on the phone. So why did you insist I drop everything just to show me the letters?"

"I don't know," Amber said.

"Yes, you do. You knew once I saw that face that I wouldn't let up. You knew I would needle you until you relented and decided to adopt the child."

"Maybe," Amber admitted.

"That's not going to happen," Robin said, surprising her.

"I see..."

"No, you don't see," Robin said, cutting her off. "The only thing you see is your own pain. Your husband was a dick. He's dead. Get over it. This child has done nothing wrong other than being born. He is not his father. He is not going to throw your love away. If you can't see that, it's on you. That is all I am going to say on the matter. I am not going to pressure you into doing the right thing and then have you throw it back in my face the first time the two of you have a mother-son fight. And you will; all mothers fight with their children at some time or other, but it won't mean he doesn't love you. It will only mean you have a normal relationship."

"I knew I could count on you not to sugarcoat the situation," Amber said, wiping tears that had formed in her eyes.

"Another bit of advice."

"Yes?"

"If you love your husband, you need to trust him. Keeping things from him is a sure way of causing a lot of pain."

Amber knew the comment was directed at the fact that Robin herself had been kept in the dark until this point. "I'm sorry I hurt you," she said sincerely.

"I'll live...but don't let it happen again," Robin said, handing her a napkin. "Now wipe your face. Your mascara is running and you look like hell."

"Gee, thanks," Amber said, taking the napkin.

"What are friends for?" Robin said, smiling.

Chapter Four

Dalton trailed a hand across the rump of the bay mare. "You did a fine job, Mama," he said, eying the two-day-old filly at her side. Even though she was born early, the filly was already straying short distances, then racing back, hiding beneath her mother. Sticking out her head, the filly eyed Dalton inquisitively.

"You're going to be a dandy," Dalton said, reaching a hand to the filly, who backed further beneath the sturdy mare. Dalton thought about naming her but decided to wait and let Amber do it. She'd been out-of-sorts lately; maybe naming the filly would help to bring her out of her funk. It wasn't lost on him that the anniversary of her husband's death was near. He'd mourned his own wife for years; granted, their situations had been greatly different – he had actually been in love with his wife and she had loved him. He smiled, picturing his late wife, happy he could now do so without feeling like his heart would never heal. While he still loved her, a good deal of time had passed since her death, and he had Amber to fill the void.

Amber was still in the early stages of her loss. Maybe she needed a distraction, something that would take her mind off things. He thought about the new barn in the west field. It was getting near completion, and he'd planned to surprise her with it when fully finished, but maybe if she had something else to occupy her mind, it would help to brighten her mood. It would still be a surprise, just one given sooner than expected. Amber hadn't been riding long – if he hurried, he could catch her. They could ride to the construction site, where he would tell her of his master plan. He rushed to the barn to saddle his horse, a smile lighting his face as he anticipated his wife's reaction.

* * *

Amber rode her painted horse along the wooded trail, allowing the reins to remain loose, letting the horse set the pace. They'd traveled the trails so many times, the horse knew the way, following the well-worn paths that would eventually circle and lead them back to the main barn. It had been two days since Robin had called her on her selfishness, and still Amber had not broached the subject with Dalton. Amber felt certain that Dalton knew something was bothering her, but he had not asked her what it was. The anniversary of Jeff's death was only a few days away, so he probably thought she was experiencing a feeling of melancholy. She felt further guilt at not telling him the truth. Jeff was gone; good riddance to him.

It was not the man who invaded her thoughts; it was what he'd left behind.

As she rode, she thought of Daxton, his image tugging at her heartstrings. At first, she had rejected the idea of adopting Jeff's love child, but since her discussion with Robin, the boy occupied her every thought. With the child came images of his mother. Anger bubbled as she pictured the woman stopping in front of her in the funeral home, her smug face glaring at her as if it were Amber who'd betrayed her. Then she remembered the same broken-hearted woman confronting her in the parking lot – screaming at her – before displaying her stomach, overstretched and heavy with child – a child fathered by the husband whose funeral she'd just sat through. Well, at least that had explained the divorce papers she'd gotten hours earlier. Therein lay the problem: how could she adopt the child of two people who had caused her so much pain? It was the same fear she shared with Robin. What if she took out her anger and hurt on the innocent boy? Amber's horse stiffened, bringing her out of her musings. Just as she was questioning what was wrong, the horse squealed its distress. Amber reached for the slack reins, but it was too late. The horse reared, tossing her off before she could grab hold of the saddle horn. She landed with a thud and managed to roll out of the way just as the horse's hooves came down inches from where she fell. The horse squealed once more before shying and running back in the direction they'd just come. Still dazed, Amber froze when she saw the cause of the horse's distress. A large snake curled on a rock beside the path, probably lured out of its nest by the warm spring day. Just when she'd decided that the black snake was not poisonous, she heard her name called from a distance.

"I'm over here," she yelled in return.

Dalton raced up on his black gelding, leading Amber's painted mare, who was still voicing her displeasure. He slid off his horse and hurried to her side. "Are you all right? What happened?" he asked, scooping her into his trembling arms.

"Snake," she said, wincing.

"Did it bite you?" Dalton asked.

"No, it just scared Wish. I wasn't paying attention and she threw me. I'm okay. Just a bit sore is all," Amber reassured him.

Dalton helped her up, then stayed close as he led the jittery horses past the snake, who remained sleeping, oblivious to the trouble its presence had caused.

"You can ride double with me," Dalton said, helping her onto his horse. "It'll give your mare a chance to calm down."

Amber allowed him to help her onto his horse, knowing he would not take no for an answer. Besides, she welcomed his reassuring embrace as he mounted behind her, his left arm circling her protectively as they rode.

"You sure you're okay?" he asked when she shifted in the saddle.

"I'm sure," she assured him. "I may need a full body massage later, though."

"Just try and stop me," he said, nibbling her ear.

She leaned into him, enjoying the closeness.

"Where are we going?" Amber asked when Dalton veered from the path.

"I just wanted to check something in the west field. Unless you're not feeling up to the ride," he said, reconsidering.

"I'm fine, Dalton," she assured him.

When they topped the hill, she was surprised to see a huge new barn. One large enough to hold quite a few horses. It was not like Dalton to keep secrets from her. *No, it is you who keeps secrets from him,* she thought as guilt washed over her anew.

"A new barn?" she asked, trying to keep her emotions at bay.

"Yes."

"It's huge. I thought you liked to keep the horses close to the house," she remarked, surprised.

Dalton kissed the top of her head. "I do, but I'm having it built specially for you."

She laughed. "Why do I need a barn?"

"For the kids," Dalton said as he brought the horses to a stop a short distance from the new structure.

Amber was confused. "Why do Julie and Katie need a barn?"

"Not those kids. The kids in our future," Dalton said, slipping off the horse and helping her to the ground.

Amber studied his face. How could he possibly know where her thoughts had been of late?

He spoke before she had a chance to ask. "When I met you, you were volunteering for a program that allowed special needs children to ride horses."

"That's right. It was the Sunshine Riders," she said.

"You've seemed to be unhappy lately, and I thought that maybe if you had an outlet that it would bring the smile back to your face. You can call the place anything you'd like. We can also offer riding lessons if you want. There is enough room inside to have a full arena, and we'll build an outside arena as well."

Amber felt her heart quicken. Did this man's kindness have no boundaries? He was always giving her gifts and doing thoughtful little things that showed her how much he cared for her, and yet she did not show him the same courtesy. She suddenly felt as if she did not deserve his love. Overcome with emotion, tears welled in her eyes, pooling until at last they spilt over and trickled down her cheeks.

Dalton's brows knitted as he wiped at the tears. "You don't like it?"

"No, I mean, I do, but that's not what's wrong," she said on a sob.

"Then you are hurt," he said anxiously. "Where? Should I call an ambulance?"

"No, I'm not in pain. Not much anyway," she said, shaking her head. She was sore, getting sorer by the minute, but her physical aches were nothing compared to the emotional pain she harbored. She had to tell him. Suddenly, for the first time since meeting Dalton, she was afraid. Afraid that he might not like the person she'd become – a person that had allowed an innocent child to suffer because of her insecurities. "I need to tell you something," she said hesitantly.

"I'm listening," he said softly.

"Not here. I'd like to go back to the house and take a hot bath. Then we can talk."

Emotions floated over Dalton's face – confusion, fear, concern – until at last, he spoke. "Whatever you have to tell me can wait until we get home," he said at last.

She smiled, grateful that he did not push the issue. She let go of a new stream of tears as he helped her onto her now calm horse, wishing he would have insisted they double up once more. One last chance to be close before her words pushed him away. They rode in silence, each absorbed in their own thoughts until they finally reached the house.

Jake met them as they neared the barn and waited for both to dismount. "Hey, boss, how was the ride?"

"Amber's horse got spooked by a snake and threw her. Make sure you check her over for any injuries," Dalton said.

"No kidding? Are you all right, Miss Amber?" Jake asked.

"I'm fine, Jake; it was my fault. I wasn't paying attention to my surroundings," she said, passing him the reins. She was almost surprised when Dalton took her hand and walked with her to the house. Guilt had had him packing her bags already. They entered through the back, bypassing the main living area and heading up the back stairs of the enormous house.

"Grab yourself something comfortable to wear, and I'll run you some bathwater," Dalton said, kissing her on top of her head.

Amber sighed as she turned to her closet. She picked out a pair of lounge pants and a top and was turning to leave when she noticed the lid removed from one of her shoeboxes. Panic engulfed her as she reached for the box.

Empty!

Her stomach knotted as she ran from the room and down the hall to find her daughter.

Julie's back was to her as she entered the room.

"I love you," Amber said.

Julie spun around, her eyes blazing. "How can you say that?"

Amber fought the urge to run to her daughter and wrap her arms around her.

Julie stood staring, nostrils flaring, eyes filling with tears. Amber could see her shivering. Amber took a tentative step and reached for her daughter's hand, which was snatched away before contact was made. Amber had a sinking feeling her newly found happiness was suddenly slipping through her hands.

"Julie, baby, you need to talk to me."

Tears trickled down Julie's face, but she made no move to wipe them. "Why didn't you leave me?"

Amber struggled to appear calmer than she felt. "Leave you where, baby?"

"When Dad died, why didn't you leave me?"

"Sweetheart, you're not making any sense. Where do you think I should have left you?"

Julie narrowed her eyes. "In foster care!"

"You found the letters."

Julie's lip trembled.

"I was looking for a pair of shoes to wear with the new dress you bought me. I opened the shoebox and saw the letters. I didn't mean to, but I saw they were postmarked from Alliance. They looked so important. Only it...my brother isn't important to you, is he?" she asked on a fresh wave of tears.

Amber wanted to be angry that Julie had invaded her privacy, but now was not the time. "Julie, you don't understand."

"Yes, I do. He's just a little boy, Mom. His mom is dying, and he needs a family. But since you hate his dad, you can't love him. So if you can't love him...how can you love me?" she asked on a sob.

"Julie, you are just upset. You are my daughter. Have I ever done anything to make you think I didn't love you?"

Julie batted at the tears. "Not until now."

Pain filled Amber's heart. "Oh, Julie, you know that's not true."

"Do I? He's my little brother, Mom. We have the same dad. Other than my height, I look like Dad. How can you hate my brother and not hate me?"

Amber bristled at that. "You are putting words into my mouth. I do not hate Daxton. I've never even met the child."

Julie's lips quivered again. "Neither have I. He's my brother, Mom, and he's so little. If you won't take care of him, then send me to foster care so that I can."

"Julie, it doesn't work like that. You have a family. People don't just drop children off in foster care for no reason."

Julie glared at her. "You did," she said coldly.

"Julie, that's not fair. This is not my fault. I am not Daxton's mother."

"No, but Daxton and I have the same dad," Julie repeated. "What if Daxton had been your son, and I was the one being sent to foster care? Then would you just leave me there?"

Amber was at a loss for words. It was not the same, and she knew it, but try telling that to a seventeen-year-old. She closed her eyes to gather her thoughts, and when she opened them, Julie was gone, the letters scattered in her wake.

Amber felt her legs trembling as she sank to the floor. She'd made such a huge mess of things. It would not be long before the rest of her world shattered around her. She was still sobbing, letters clutched in her hands, when Dalton found her and gathered her into his arms.

"It's all right, Amber Mae. Whatever is going on, we'll get through it," Dalton cooed as he carried her down the hallway. He sounded so sure of himself.

If only she could be so sure.

Chapter Five

Amber stayed in the bath until the water grew cold, going over the events of the last four years. Finally, shivering, she left the confines of the large soaking tub. As she opened the bathroom door, she saw Dalton waiting in the sitting room that adjoined the bedroom, his face devoid of all expression. The couch where they generally sat beside one another remained empty; he'd taken one of the chairs instead. She took his lead, sitting in the empty chair next to his. Her gaze fell to the envelopes on the table between the two chairs. On top of the pile rested the photo showcasing the smiling face of the child no one wanted. His green eyes seemed to be searching hers.

He would love you if you gave him a chance.

When she lifted her gaze, Dalton was staring at her. "Why?" he asked.

Why didn't I tell you? Why didn't I trust you enough to ask your opinion? Why didn't I give you the option of saying yes or no? There were so many "why" questions, she didn't know which he was asking. "I don't know," she said, answering all of the ones she could think of.

"Do you love me?" Dalton asked.

She felt her eyes fly open in response to this unexpected question. "I love you more than I could ever express."

"When we met, we had an instant connection. We both told each other things we had not shared with anyone else. So why didn't you think you could share this with me?"

"I was afraid," Amber said truthfully.

"Of me?"

"No. Yes..." she replied.

"I don't understand. Have I ever done anything to make you not trust me? Have I ever been cruel to you in any way?"

"It's not that, Dalton."

"Then what is it, Amber? Did you think that I wouldn't want the child?" he asked, leaning closer.

"I didn't want to burden you with another one of Jeff's children. You took Julie in and accepted her as your own. Never once have I ever heard you refer to her as your stepdaughter. But I didn't think it would be fair to ask you to take on another burden."

His face turned red. "A burden? Do you think that is what Julie is to me?"

"No... of course not. I just didn't want you to see Jeff every time you looked into his face."

Dalton picked up the photo, staring at it. "Are you talking about me or you?"

"What do you mean?"

"I didn't know Jeff. While I've seen pictures, I never met the man. I think it's you that is afraid. You're afraid of what you see when you look at this little boy." He turned the photo so that she could see it. "What do you see, Amber? Tell me."

"I see a child," she said lamely.

"That is a bunch of hogwash, and you know it." He pushed the photo in front of her face. "You see a bastard child who tore your insides out. You see a woman who shamed you in front of your daughter and the whole town. You see your in-laws, who never gave a damn about you or the daughter you gave birth to. You see a husband who married you because you were pregnant but who never loved you."

Tears ran down her cheeks. Tears of shame because she knew everything he said was true.

He pulled the photo away, walked a short distance, and retrieved a frame from the wall before returning to his chair. "Do you know what I see when I look at the picture, Amber?" he asked more gently.

Not trusting herself to speak, she simply shook her head.

"I see Julie," he said, showing her the framed photo he'd taken from the wall. He placed the small snapshot of Daxton within the frame alongside his sister. As he did, Amber's tears subsided. Dalton was right. She no longer saw Jeff or all the pain he'd caused. She was seeing two children who looked so much alike, it was clear they were siblings.

"Do you ever see Jeff when you look at Julie?" Dalton asked, placing both photos on the small round table.

"Of course; she looks a lot like her father," Amber said, wiping the moisture from her face.

"And when you see him in her, does it make you hate her? Or wish she hadn't been born?" he inquired.

"No, of course not," Amber said truthfully.

"Then why do you think it would be any different with that little boy?"

"But what if I end up blaming him?" Amber asked on a sob.

"Blaming him for what, Amber? The way I see it, you should be thanking that little boy."

She looked at Dalton in question. "How so?"

"Had Jeff not have died in that wreck, that little guy there would have saved you. Jeff would still have been out of the picture, and you would have been free to be with me. Don't you see, Amber, that little guy was sent into the world to help you heal your heart, not break it."

Amber felt a glimmer of hope bubbling inside of her. What he was saying was making so much sense. "So you wouldn't have a problem adopting him?"

"Do you mean can I love a boy who has already made me the happiest man on earth?" Dalton asked.

"You sure have a wonderful way of looking at things," Amber said, batting at newly shed tears. "'Does this mean you are not mad at me?"

He clasped her hand in his. "Amber, I was never mad at you. I know how much the guy hurt you, but you need to remember I am not that guy. I love you – have loved you from the first moment I saw you. We jumped in with both feet, and I don't regret one single second of it, but you need to remember we are a team. If one of us has a problem, we both have a problem. No more secrets," he said, standing and drawing her into him.

44

Dalton was right; she'd allowed the secret to gnaw at her until the weight of it nearly festered out of control. *And look at how easy it was to fix. Wait does that mean we are going to adopt the child?*

"So what now?" she asked hopefully.

Dalton smiled a wide smile, the creases near his eyes crinkling, lending to his boyish charm.

"Now you get that attorney on the phone and tell him we are on the way to pick up our son," he said, kissing her.

As he pulled away, his face took on a serious expression. "But before we go, there is a fence to mend."

"A fence? Can't Carl or one of the ranch hands take care of that?"

"Not this time," Dalton said, plucking the framed photo of Julie from the table and handing it to her. "This is a fence that needs a woman's touch."

Amber took the picture from him. The small photo of Daxton was still tucked securely within the frame. She studied the pair more closely, amazed that now when she looked at the chubby little cheeks, she saw Julie at the same age smiling up at her. She pulled both pictures to her chest, hugging them tightly. "Thank you," she said, smiling up at Dalton.

He traced his fingers along her cheekbone. "For what, darlin'?"

"For loving me enough to tell me the truth," Amber replied, leaning into his touch.

* * *

Finding Julie took some doing. It was only after she'd searched the house that Amber decided to check the barns. A feat, given that the fall from the horse was starting to catch up with her. Amber finally found her in the back barn sitting on the haystack next to Travis. The two were deep in discussion, and Amber slowed her pace, not wanting to interrupt them.

"Give your mother a chance," Travis said.

"Why should I?" Julie said hotly. "It's not fair, Grandpa. What if it would have been me?"

Amber waited as her father gathered his words. "There is no way your mom is going to let your brother stay in foster care. She just needs some time to gather her courage. Your grandma raised her to do the right thing. She's been through a lot, but she'll come around."

Julie's voice brightened. "Do you really think so?"

"I do," he said with a nod.

"What if she waits too long and he gets adopted by someone else?" Julie asked.

"Those things take time. Now that your mother knows that you know, she will see that things are put right. Has she ever let you down?" Travis asked.

"No," Julie answered.

"And she won't this time. Now, why don't we mosey back to the house and see if we can talk some sense into the woman."

"That won't be necessary," Amber said, approaching the pair. "Dalton and I have already agreed to call Mr. Grether and have him make the arrangements. Then we are going to go get your brother."

Julie leapt from the haystack and threw herself into Amber's arms. "Oh my God! Really? When are we leaving?"

"Easy, kiddo," Amber said, gritting her teeth against the pain of being jostled. "Your dad," she said, using the name Julie now used in referring to Dalton, "and I still have to work things out. I'm not sure who all is going."

"No way I'm staying home!" Julie said, pushing out of Amber's embrace. "I'm not waiting a minute longer to meet my little brother." With that, she turned, running towards the house.

Amber sat on the haystack next to her father. "I was worried she'd run away."

"Naw, I found her out here crying her eyes out," Travis said with a sigh.

"I've sure made a mess of things, haven't I?" Amber said, her sigh matching his.

"You just got dealt a raw hand, little girl," Travis said, placing a rough hand on her knee.

"I used to think so too," she said, resting her hand on his.

"I'm sorry I let you down," he said without looking at her. "When your mother died, I was in so much pain, then every time I looked at you, I saw her, which is why I kept pushing you away. The bottle helped to squelch that pain, and after a while, I couldn't function without that first drink of the day, which led to another and then another."

Amber felt the fear bubbling once more, the fear of hurting the child who needed her so.

"What is it that ails you, Pumpkin?"

"I'm afraid, Dad. What if I can't love the child that caused me so much pain?"

He turned to her with tears in his eyes. "Is that what you think? That I didn't love you?"

"Isn't that what you just said?"

"God, no! I loved you so much. I was afraid of hurting you more than you were already hurting. After your mother died, I gave up. I would have given anything to have died when she did. Watching her dwindle away like that tore my heart out. I loved your mother, and a big piece of me did die that day."

"Thank you for talking with Julie," she said, swiping at tears that trailed down her face.

"No, it is I who needs to thank you," he said, lowering his eyes to the ground. "Thank you for giving me a chance to be in her life after all I put you through."

"I'm afraid I can't take the credit for that," Amber said softly. "I didn't want you here. It was Dalton who convinced me to give you another chance."

His eyes met hers. "I know, I overheard the conversation, but in the end, it was you that agreed. It was clear that if you'd said no that he would have honored your wishes. You have a good heart, my daughter. If you can forgive an old man that abandoned you when you needed him most, you'll have no problem loving a child that only wants the same in return."

Amber wanted to reach out to him and hug him like she'd done as a little girl. Instead, she leaned into his shoulder and drew comfort in that. As much as she wanted to open her heart to him, she held back. He'd broken her trust too many times and she just wasn't ready to take that step.

Chapter Six

With the decision made to adopt Daxton, the house was alive with preparations. Amber's call to her attorney, Mr. Grether, had started the proceedings. However, things were not moving as quickly as they'd planned. Daxton's foster family was fighting the child's removal from their home. Mr. Grether assured Amber that getting the child placed into her and Dalton's care would only take a few days, especially since the child's blood relatives had not given up full custody when placing him in foster care. It was all a mere matter of formalities, the attorney had assured them. In the meantime, Amber and Dalton were busy fixing up Katie Mae's old nursery. The room had sat vacant since Katie Mae moved to the larger room next to it shortly after they were married. Gone were the pink walls, updated with a fresh new coat of light blue. Julie proved to be quite the budding artist, painting one wall with clouds, mountains, and a Wild West open range. Jake had joined in on the activities, amazing everyone by adding some pretty realistic-looking horses. He'd painted two to match Amber and Dalton's horses, promising to paint another once they picked out a horse for Daxton. Dalton had looked online and found a twin bed in the shape of an old covered wagon, which was scheduled for delivery the following week.

Barbara entered the room, carrying a bundle of fabric. "All finished!" she said, unfolding what proved to be cowboy curtains.

"They're perfect!" Amber said, helping her hold them up to the window.

"I sure hope that boy likes horses," Maggie said as she brushed into the room followed by Katie Mae.

"Of course he'll like horses," Dalton said, following on her heels. "Whatcha got there, Little Bit?" he asked, turning to his youngest daughter.

"Letters," she said, laying them out on the floor to spell the word READ. "Miss Maggie helped me paint them. They go over my brother's bookshelves. I'm going to give him some of my toys too!"

Amber felt the palpable joy that resonated through the room. The whole family was coming together to make Daxton's homecoming a happy one. It pained her to know that she'd nearly cheated her family out of the gift they would soon receive. It was as if the whole family was pregnant and waiting for the delivery date. Each person would get something to fill a void they didn't know was missing: a son, brother, grandson. How selfish she'd been. Adopting the boy was the right thing to do.

Then why was she still feeling uneasy?

Dalton came up behind her, wrapping his arms solidly around her. "Not having second thoughts, are you?" he whispered.

"No, of course not," Amber said, quelling her fears. She watched as everyone placed the finishing touches on the room. "Just feeling a bit guilty for not..."

"What's done is done. We move on from here, Amber Mae."

Amber leaned into his embrace as they stood watching Jake show Julie how to draw tumbleweeds. Julie giggled and batted doe eyes at Jake as he took her hand, guiding it along the wall.

"Um, I think we may have a problem," she whispered.

"Maybe I should get him gelded the next time Doc Taylor is out this way," Dalton said, watching the pair.

Amber stifled a laugh, picturing the vet performing such services.

"Might see if you can get a two for one deal," she said, nodding towards the window where her father was helping Barbara hang the curtains. "Is it me or does the house feel overly amorous today?"

"Darlin', it's springtime in Kentucky. The weather is warming, and everything and everyone's feeling their oats," Dalton said, nuzzling her neck.

"You included?" Amber asked, enjoying the closeness.

"I don't need warm weather to tell me how much I want you," Dalton whispered.

Closing her eyes, Amber let out a contented sigh.

"Oh for heaven's sakes, I feel like I've stepped into a bad episode of *The Love Connection*," Maggie said, drawing everyone's attention. "There's enough sexual tension in this room to make an old woman blush. Are we decorating a nursery or doing a mating ritual? You two," she said, pointing at Julie and Jake, "put some distance between you."

With that, the two teens blushed and moved away from each other.

"And you both are old enough to know better," she said, turning her attention to Barbara and Travis, who, ignoring her rant, continued to fiddle with the curtains.

"As for the two of you," she said, pointing at Dalton and Amber, "take your shenanigans elsewhere."

Amber felt Dalton bristle. "Now, Maggie, I'll have you know there are no shenanigans going on between my wife and me. I was merely nuzzling her neck, which I assure you was done with the lady's sincere permission."

"Well, I'd think you of all people would want to set a good example," Maggie said firmly.

Dalton backed away from Amber. "Of course, what was I thinking? How dare I share a tender moment with my bride and let my family see how much she means to me."

Maggie shook her head, the corners of her mouth twitching, betraying her good humor. She walked to where Dalton and Amber were standing. Nodding towards Julie and Jake, she lowered her voice. "You remember that when those two start showing their affection. You mark my words, young man. It's only a matter of time. I've seen the way those two look at each other."

Before either Amber or Dalton could respond, Maggie turned her attention to Katie Mae, who'd just come back in the room with a handful of stuffed animals.

"Katie, let's go up in the attic and see if we can find some of your old storybooks for the little one. Someone has to protect the innocent," she said, casting a despairing look at both Dalton and Amber and leading Katie Mae from the room.

"She's got a point," Amber said after they'd left the room. "Kids do tend to imitate what they see."

"Darlin', teenagers will do what comes natural whether they see it or not," Dalton said with a laugh.

"I wonder if you'd be taking this so lightly if it were Katie Mae," Amber said, then, seeing the hurt that passed over his face, she immediately regretted her words. "I'm sorry. I didn't mean to suggest that you don't love Julie the same as your own daughter."

Without a word, Dalton took her hand and led her from the room. She thought about apologizing but knew it wouldn't help. What was wrong with her lately? Why did it seem as if she were trying to push him away?

"We've been married for four years. In that time, have I ever played favorites with the girls?" he asked once they'd reached the confines of the master suite.

"No, you've been wonderful with Julie," Amber assured him.

"I've tried, Amber. I knew when I asked you to share my life that I was also taking responsibility for Julie. She is a wonderful girl, and I would never do anything to hurt her. I would also never allow anyone else hurt her. That includes Jake, who I love like a son. Jake's a great guy. A parent could not ask for anyone better to take an interest in their daughter."

"But she is only seventeen," Amber reminded him. *The same age I was when I met Jeff.*

"Which is why I plan on talking to him and letting him know that if I see any signs of inappropriate behavior, he will have to go," Dalton said, meeting her eyes.

"I'm sorry I said what I did," Amber said.

"Me too. Where is all of this coming from lately? Are you still having doubts about adopting Daxton?"

"I don't know, maybe..."

"What is it you're really afraid of, Amber?"

"I guess I'm just afraid of not being able to love him like a mother's supposed to," Amber said softly.

"Do you love Katie Mae?"

"Of course I do. I've loved Katie from the first time I saw her."

"Exactly, and yet you did not give birth to her."

"Yes, but what if that's just because she is a part of you? This child is not a part of either of us," she said, picturing the face of the woman who'd given birth to the child, a face she'd seen many times in her dreams. While she hated her husband, she also despised the child's mother, and that frightened her.

"No, but he is a part of Julie, and we both love her," Dalton reminded her.

"But what if it's not the same?"

Dalton smiled. "Darlin', you are not giving yourself enough credit. You are kind and loving, and I assure you, the second you lay eyes on that boy, you are going to laugh at all the worrying you've done."

"Do you really think so?" she asked, hoping it to be true.

He pulled her into his arms. "There's not a doubt in my mind."

She winced against his embrace.

"Are you okay?" he asked, pulling back.

"Just a bit sore still from this morning's fall."

"Maybe we should call the doctor," he said, full of concern.

"No, there's nothing broken. They would just tell me to take Motrin, which I've already done."

"Well, just the same, I insist you take the rest of the day off. Daxton's room is nearly done and the others can finish the rest."

She kissed him fully on the lips. "Why are you so good to me?"

He hugged her tenderly. "It's my job."

"You do it so well," she said.

"So do you, Amber. I know Maggie keeps the house running, but you have settled in seamlessly. You don't feel put off to have Maggie and Barbara running the house. I've never heard you try to undermine the way they do things. You've always seemed comfortable in your own skin and confident, but lately, I feel something is pulling at you. At first, I thought it was the time of year. You know, the anniversary of Jeff's death. Then I thought it was the turmoil of not telling me about Daxton. But that isn't it, is it?"

Amber felt tears well in her eyes, surprised at how fast they'd arrived.

"What is it, Amber?" Dalton asked softly.

"I feel as if I've let you down," she said, batting away the tears.

His brows knitted together. "In what way?"

"I was hoping to give you a son," she said with a sob.

His face softened. "But you are, Amber. He will be here any day."

"You don't understand," she said, blowing her nose. "Dalton, I'm afraid."

"Of what?" he asked, tilting his head.

"Jeff wanted a son, but we had a girl instead. Then he was in the process of leaving me because that woman was able to give him something I couldn't."

Dalton clenched his hands into a fist, blew out a breath, then relaxed his fingers. "I'm not a violent man, but what I wouldn't give to punch Jeff in the face for what he did to you. I'm not that guy, Amber. I married you, not a broodmare. To be perfectly honest, when I asked you to marry me, having more children never crossed my mind. We both have perfectly healthy daughters, and together we are a family. I've never pushed you into trying to become pregnant."

"But you agreed, so you must want more children."

"Of course I do, but it doesn't mean I'd ever leave you if we don't. You've been living with something that was not your fault for way too long, Amber. You did nothing wrong. As for you not becoming pregnant, you know as well as I do that is my fault. Stop blaming yourself for everything bad that happens and start living the happy life you deserve. We can be happy even if we never have any more children. But to be happy, you need to stop living in the past."

"Do you still want to adopt Daxton?"

"Of course I do. But only if doing so will make you happy. If bringing that child into the house is going to cause you more heartache, then no."

Amber took a deep breath. She was feeling so much better about the decision after telling him her fears. "That baby needs us, and I think we have a lot to offer him," she said, meaning it.

"Just to be clear, when I found out my wife was pregnant, I didn't care what sex the baby was as long as the child was healthy. I'm not telling you anything you don't already know, but your ex was a scumbag, and I'm pretty sure that even if he did not get a girl pregnant, he would have found a reason to leave. I'll always be grateful for Katie Mae, but I would have loved her even if she'd been a boy and just the same if we would have adopted her."

Amber watched as sadness crossed over his face. Dalton's wife, Mary Katherine, had died shortly after giving birth to their only child, having been diagnosed with bone cancer only after learning she was pregnant, refusing treatment for the sake of the child they'd waited so long to have.

She reached for him. "I'm sorry I made you remember. I know how much you must miss her."

"I do," he admitted. "But I'm sure Mary Katherine is watching over us and would be the first to tell us that we are doing the right thing. The boy needs us, Amber, and near as I can tell, we need him just as much."

"How do you mean?"

"I think he will be just the thing to keep this family on their toes. Besides, Julie will be so busy watching over the little guy that she won't have time for a budding romance with Jake."

Amber laughed. "Well, that's a plus."

"Sure is. Besides, I'd hate to have to fire the lad. He is such a good horseman."

"But you would," Amber said, knowing it was true.

"I'd kick him to the curb so fast he wouldn't know how he got there," Dalton said with a wink.

"You're such a good dad, Dalton," Amber said.

"And you are a wonderful mom. You're going to be okay, Amber Mae, and more than that, this family is going to be okay. I know you don't have a lot of experience with sharing the load, but that's what families do; they look after each other. If at any time you think you need a break, just ask. One of us will step in and help. I know that for the most part, you raised Julie on your own, but just remember you are not alone. We're all in this together. We've got your back."

Amber smiled a warm smile. "You have a wonderful way of chasing away all of my fears."

"Then I'm doing my job," Dalton said, his eyes twinkling. "How about we go see how the others are faring?"

Amber's cell phone rang. She looked at the caller ID and smiled, knowing she was finally ready to bring Daxton home where he belonged.

"It's Mr. Grether," she said, answering the call. "Hello?" Amber felt her heart tighten as she listened to what her attorney had to say.

"What's wrong?" Dalton asked the second she ended the call.

"Mr. Grether said the foster mother has disappeared." Amber watched as the fear on his face mimicked what she felt.

"And?" The word came out as a whisper.

"Dalton, she's taken our son!" she said with a sob.

Chapter Seven

A lull had settled over the ranch, everyone speaking in hushed tones, yet no one voicing the reason for the disturbance in the normally cheerful home. The door to the nursery remained closed since getting the news; all remaining updates left unfinished. Amber continued to blame herself for not taking action sooner, and try as he might, Dalton couldn't seem to pull her from her funk. As Dalton neared the room, he noticed a light under the doorway. Taking a breath, he opened the door and quietly entered. The wagon bed had arrived a few days earlier and stood leaning against the far wall. The mural remained unfinished, as though the horses were waiting for a foal that never arrived. Even though the room had sat empty for nearly four years, it never felt as empty as it did at that moment. He'd always dreamed of a house full of children, never imagining that he would not be able to physically fulfill that dream. He'd accepted that, even as Amber tried to prove the doctors wrong. Deep down, he'd hoped it would be different with Amber. That maybe their love would be strong enough to produce a child, even though his sperm count was low. When Amber agreed to adopt Daxton, he was ecstatic, not only because he was getting a son. That was a bonus, but the real joy was in fulfilling his dream of having a large family and being able to share that joy with a woman who meant the world to him. Now that dream seemed to be teetering on a shaky ledge.

He turned to where Amber sat silently rocking in the rocking chair. How many nights had he sat in that same chair, clinging to the child that was his only remaining link to his beloved Mary Katherine?

The rocking stopped, making him wonder if she'd heard him. When she didn't move, he crossed to where Amber was sitting. Her jet black hair cascaded around her shoulders as she sat holding a stuffed horse. Dalton bent and kissed the top of her head, startling her in the process.

"Sorry. I didn't mean to scare you," he said, rubbing the tension from her shoulders. "What are you doing sitting in here all alone?"

"Just thinking," she replied softly.

"You mean beating yourself up."

He watched as Amber rolled her neck to relieve the tension before answering him.

"It's hard not to. Everyone seems so sad, and this room," she waved her arms, "feels so empty."

I understand completely.

"The room's been empty for years, but I know what you're saying," Dalton said before she could explain.

Amber ran her fingers through the horse's mane. It was a small, stuffed black and white horse she'd ordered from the internet the evening they'd decided to adopt the child. Unable to sleep, she'd tiptoed out of the room and scoured the Internet until she saw a floppy horse that reminded her of her own mare. The moment she'd seen it, she knew it was what she was looking for and bought it in hopes that it would somehow give her and the child a connection. She'd returned to bed, and after finally falling asleep, she'd dreamed of a small, sandy-haired child running around playing with what he referred to as *Mommy's horse.*

"I waited too long," she said softly.

Dalton sighed. They'd had this same conversation multiple times over the last week. "We can't change the past, darlin'. We've done all we can, but one thing's for sure, sitting in this room thinking about all that you think you should have done is not going to help find him."

She looked up at him, her deep brown eyes filled with a sorrow that nearly crushed his soul.

"Still nothing from Jackson?" she asked.

Dalton had hired a private investigator within minutes of hearing that Daxton had gone missing. That had been five days ago. While Jackson hadn't found the child, all signs currently showed that the mother's disappearance was not well planned. The husband still went to work every day, and while he'd had no physical contact with his wife, there were indications that he had been in contact with her. There had been multiple sightings of the woman and child, and in each case, Jackson missed apprehending them by just a few moments. So far, all sightings were in the town where the family lived. Most likely they were being hidden by well-intentioned relatives until the family could come up with a legal option. Both Mr. Grether and Dalton's family attorney had assured them that there were no legal channels that would allow the foster family to keep the child, providing, of course, they could find him in the first place. As long as the husband didn't disappear, Dalton remained hopeful they would find Daxton. Jackson had a man keeping the guy under constant surveillance, so the chances of him disappearing were slim.

"They will find him," Dalton said with more confidence than he felt.

"I hope so," Amber replied.

"Try not to worry. Remember, this is not a random kidnapping. Daxton knows them, and they appear to love him, or they wouldn't have taken off with him. Most likely they are just buying time."

"You mean trying to figure out a way to keep him."

"Put that thought out of your mind, Amber Mae. We have the law on our side."

"I know, but I can't help it. Sitting around doing nothing is maddening. I want to go and look for him." As if making up her mind, Amber sprang from the rocking chair.

"Now hold on, Amber Mae. You can't just go trailing around the countryside looking for them."

"Not the countryside. Jackson said they seem to be staying with family. I can just go knock on a couple of doors and…"

"And, what? Get yourself killed?"

"This isn't a TV show. It's real life. You said it before: they are not bad people; they are desperate."

"Yes, and desperate people tend to do desperate things."

"I have to do something, Dalton. Besides, I won't be alone. I will… I will take Robin with me!"

"Oh great, nothing could possibly be wrong with that scenario. It will be Thelma and Louise all over again."

"Only I will be driving, we won't pick up Brad Pitt, and there are no cliffs in that part of Michigan to drive off of."

"Well, that makes me feel better."

"So I can go?" she asked, looking hopeful.

He ran his hand through his hair. It was against his better judgment, but he knew firsthand how frustrating it was not to be able to do anything. It would get her out of the house for a few days. She would have Robin to keep an eye on her. Maybe the trip would do some good, and hopefully, lift her spirits a bit.

"I guess it wouldn't hurt. If anything, it would put you in the area if…when," Dalton corrected, "Jackson finds the boy."

"Exactly," Amber said, brightening. "I'll call Robin."

Dalton pulled her into his arms. "Promise me you will coordinate everything with Jackson. I will call and let him know you are heading that way, but when you get there, you need to call and let him know you have arrived."

"I promise," she said, smiling for the first time in days.

He held her a few more seconds before releasing her. "I would feel much better if I was going with you."

She laughed. "No, you would feel much better if I were staying home."

"True, but I also know you will not rest until that little boy is safe and home where he belongs. I'm proud of you, Amber Mae."

Her brow furrowed. "Proud? Why?"

"Look at you, darlin'. Last week, you had no intention of bringing that child into our home. Now you are ready to move mountains to get him here. You are a good mother, and this proves you will be just as fierce when it comes to our son."

She smiled. "Our son. I like the sound of that."

He placed his palm against her face. "So do I, Amber Mae. So do I."

Chapter Eight

Amber and Robin arrived in Larrimore, Michigan just before three in the afternoon. A medium-size town on the outskirts of Detroit, Larrimore was host to many residents that enjoyed low housing costs and even lower crime statistics than the big city it bordered. While the town was not large by big-city standards, it offered a much larger footprint than most of the outlying towns.

Amber gaped out the window as Robin maneuvered Amber's Durango through heavy traffic. "Sheesh, I didn't realize the town was this large. No wonder the private investigator hasn't been able to find Daxton."

"It's close to Detroit. What were you expecting?" Robin asked.

"I guess I wasn't. I mean, I guess I thought it would be just a quaint town like Alliance," Amber said, speaking of the small Michigan town where they once lived.

"Yeah, we could have knocked on every door in town in a single day," Robin agreed.

"If only…" Amber said, picturing the town she'd moved to upon marrying Jeff and lived in up until marrying Dalton four years prior. She and Robin could, and often did, run the perimeters of the town. A person could drive up and down every street within city limits in a matter of minutes. "It would have been easier to find the boy if they'd put him into foster care in Alliance."

"I'm surprised they put him in foster care this close to where the mother lived."

Amber glanced at her friend. "Why is that?"

"Too easy for the parents to come and kidnap the children."

"As opposed to the foster parent trying to kidnap the child," Amber said heatedly. "Seriously, have you ever heard of someone doing that?"

"No, not until now," Robin said as she changed lanes. "Listen, I don't mind driving around and looking for the kid, but do you have an actual destination in mind?"

"No. I guess I didn't put a lot of thought into this. I just wanted to feel like I was doing something. You know, using the force and all. A mother always knows where her child is, right?"

Robin laughed and shot Amber a disbelieving look. "Good one. I gave birth to three kids and have never known what they are up to from one moment to the next. Now tell me how you really plan on finding the kid."

Amber sighed. "I have no freaking clue."

This produced another chuckle. "Okay, now that I believe. Any idea where the foster family lived?"

"Nope."

"Worked?"

"Nope?"

"Okay, so at least we have a picture of the foster parents from the Amber alert."

Amber laughed.

"Care to share the joke?"

"It is just that when Katie heard about the Amber alert, she was pretty incensed. She thought that since it was Daxton that was missing and not me, they should have issued a Daxton alert. I still don't think she realizes they always call them Amber alerts."

"Oh, that is priceless."

"I agree. Got to love kids; they have no filter. Hey, pull in there," Amber said, pointing.

Robin eased the SUV into the McDonald's parking lot.

"What are we doing?"

"Coming up with a plan. Any ideas?"

"This is your rodeo, sister. I'm just driving the getaway car."

"Yeah, about that. If Dalton asks, I drove."

Robin frowned. "Dalton has a problem with my driving?"

"No, but I promised him we wouldn't do the whole Thelma and Louise thing and drive off a cliff."

"No worries; this area is as flat as they come."

"I also promised Dalton we would not pick up Brad Pitt."

"Bummer."

Amber smiled, swiped her cell phone, scrolled through until she found the number she was looking for, and pressed dial. "I'm calling Jackson."

"Does he look like Brad Pitt?"

The in-dash Bluetooth screen showed a call in progress. Amber motioned for Robin to be quiet as the call was answered. They heard shouting coming through the speakers in the dashboard.

"Hello? Jackson, this is Amber. Are you there? Hello?" Amber waited but heard nothing. She looked at the screen and realized the call was dropped.

"Well, that was weird," Robin said.

"It sounded like he was arguing with someone. Do you think maybe he found them? Should I call him back?"

"Give him a minute. He sounded a little busy. You wait for the call. I'm going to run in and grab us each coffee. You want anything else?"

"No, coffee will be fine. I think I'll drive for a bit." They each got out, stretched, and Amber walked to the driver's side door.

"I'll be right back," Robin said, heading towards the building.

Amber pushed the button and waited for the seat and mirrors to adjust to her saved setting. She looked at her phone to make sure the volume was turned up as minutes seemed to slowly tick by. A silver minivan pulled into the parking space on the driver's side. Amber watched as a thin lady with short, dark hair got out of the van. Her hair was sticking out in all directions like she'd gotten dressed in a hurry. She had the look of someone who'd partied way into the night. Amber watched as the woman studied her appearance in the side mirror and gave a frustrated sigh before circling in front of the minivan. Amber noticed she had dark circles under her eyes and seemed to have the same haunted look she'd seen on her dad for years. The woman saw her staring, pulled on sunglasses, opened the door, and removed a heavy coat. "I hope you get help," Amber whispered. Her thoughts drifted to her dad and left her wondering how different her life would have been if he hadn't fallen into the bottle. She heard a commotion and looked in her side mirror. The side door was now open, and the haggard woman was struggling with a child. From what little Amber could see, she guessed the little girl was no more than four years old. The child was wearing a dress, and the mom was struggling to get a frilly hat onto her head.

"I don't blame ya, kid. That hat is hideous," Amber whispered under her breath.

"No hat!" the little girl screamed, pulling frantically at the cap.

"Yes, hat," the woman said equally as loud and pulled the hat firmly over the child's head.

Amber leaned forward to guess the age better but still couldn't see the child's face. *You need to learn to pick your battles, lady. It will be even worse when she becomes a teenager.*

"No hat! No dress!" the child screamed in return.

"Yes, dress. Yes, hat!" the woman argued.

Amber laughed. *Okay, maybe the woman has a reason for drinking this early after all.*

"If you'll be a nice little girl, Mommy will get you some French fries," the woman said in frustration.

"No mommy!" Just then, the child looked up, saw where they were, and relaxed. She pointed to the building, a smile replacing the frown. "French fries? Ketchup?"

"Yes, with ketchup," the lady agreed.

And with that, the battle of wills was over. Both mother and child walked towards the building holding hands.

Ketchup…better than whisky in the morning.

The side door opened. Robin handed a coffee cup to Amber before climbing in and closing the door. "Anything new?"

"No call from Jackson, but remind me to get some ketchup."

"Okay…"

"The lady in the minivan next to us was having a power struggle with a four-year-old, and she won by promising to let the kid have some ketchup."

"Are you sure you are ready to do the whole kid thing again?"

"I'm ready to do all of it again," Amber said longingly.

"Better you than me," Robin said, sipping her coffee.

"It's going to be different this time. With Julie, it was just me. Jeff was never home, and even when he was, he never lifted a finger to change a diaper, fix a meal, or do anything that even resembled being a dad." She put the SUV into reverse and backed out of the parking space.

"In order to do that, he would have had to have started by being a decent husband first," Robin quipped.

Amber tilted her head and spoke to the roof of the car. "Sorry, but you know you were a jerk."

Robin followed her gaze. "You just spoke to your dead husband. Should I be worried about you?"

"Not anymore." Amber laughed and pulled out into traffic.

"I'm glad you found him. Dalton," Robin clarified, then took another sip of coffee.

"I knew who you were talking about," Amber replied.

Robin had never hesitated to let Amber know she didn't approve of her late husband.

"I wish I would have known you before I married Jeff. You could have warned me about him."

Robin snorted her coffee. "Do you really think you would have listened to me?"

"No. I was a typical teen. I knew everything. Believed everything." It was true. She'd lost her mother at an early age. The loss was doubly painful as her mother's death sent her father into the thralls of alcoholism. In a way, she'd lost both parents that year. She was only just rekindling her relationship with her father.

"Thinking about your dad, aren't you?"

Amber whipped her head around in surprise. "How'd you know?"

"It's where you always go when you think about Jeff. You run to your mom, but she is not there. She's dead, so you haven't the heart to blame her for the way your life turned out. So you go to the one person that it is safe to hate. Your dad."

"I don't hate him," she lied.

"Yes you do."

"Maybe." She felt her grip tighten on the wheel. God help her, she did hate him. "If he'd been more of a father, maybe my life wouldn't have turned out the way it did."

Robin tilted the cup and drained the contents before speaking. "You don't have to worry about money. You live in a mansion, on a huge horse farm where your only job is to go horseback riding whenever you want. Oh, and you are married to the man of your dreams."

Amber turned and looked at her friend.

"Eyes on the road," Robin chided. "Listen, I'm not saying you didn't have a tough go of it. But even when the asshole wasn't there, you had it pretty easy."

Amber felt her lips tremble. "I thought you were my friend."

Robin laughed. "Well, I didn't come along on this trip because I hate you. But to be honest, I think it's high time you stop blaming everyone else for how sucky your life has been and start enjoying what you've got."

Amber opened her mouth to speak, but Robin put up her hand. "I'm not finished yet. Jeff was the slime of the earth, but think about it. If you hadn't married the fricker, you might have ended up in a humdrum marriage with three kids, four dogs, seven cats, and a husband named Steve, who is into kinky sex and wants you to call him 'big daddy.' As it is, your sucky marriage is a thing of the past, and you get to spend the rest of your life living the dream and sharing your bed with a handsome cowboy."

Amber changed lanes and waited for Robin to continue. When she did not, she opened her mouth to speak. "Steve?"

Robin shrugged. "Would you have preferred I said Fred, and that he wanted to tie you up and suck on your toes?"

Amber laughed. "No! I get the point."

Robin turned to her. "I'm not trying to beat you up here, but dang, girl, you have to stop with all these pity parties. It's not very becoming on you. And, one more thing."

Amber took in a breath. "Let me have it."

"Has your dad given you any reason to think he's been drinking again?"

"No."

"He loved your mom. I can't imagine how I would react if I lost Jack. He is my life. Maybe you really should cut him some slack. Just my opinion..."

Before Amber could respond, the dashboard lit up, showing an incoming call from Jackson. She pushed the green handset on the display. "Tell me you have good news."

"I have news. Not sure how good it is," was his reply.

"Ugh. Now what?"

When you called earlier, I was following up on a lead that the foster mom was staying at a friend's house. It took some doing, but the friend finally fessed up that they were indeed staying there and had left the house a half hour earlier. Apparently, the friend works nights, and the kid was running all over the house, keeping her awake."

Amber felt a glimmer of hope. "Did she say when they are coming back?"

"Yeah, she claimed they just went to lunch and would be back in a couple of hours."

"Then we go to the friend's house and wait," Amber said, relief filling her voice.

"That would be a waste of time," Robin countered.

"Why would you say that?" Amber said, still watching the road in front of her.

"Because if I were the friend, even if I weren't happy with the things you were doing, I'd still have your back. I would have you on speed dial and tell you not to come back to the house."

Amber caught the double-entendre. She reached over and patted Robin's hand. "And I'd listen because you are my best friend."

"Things get slightly complicated from here," Jackson said. "Turns out the foster mom is pretty smart. She has changed her appearance, and the kid may also be in disguise."

"What is he? In a Halloween costume?"

"Worse, the kid is dressed like a little girl," Jackson replied.

They went to get lunch!

Amber's heart began to race. "What were they driving?"

"A minivan. The friend claimed she couldn't remember the make or color."

"Silver Dodge! They were just at McDonald's. Dammit, he was right beside me!" she said and spun the Durango back the way they'd just come.

"Got to love the turning radius on this thing," Robin said, holding on. "You sure it was them?"

Amber related the power struggle between the woman and child. "I just assumed it was a little girl giving her mom a hard time."

"I'm on my way. I'll call the local police and have them meet us there," Jackson shouted into the phone.

"Yeah, and while you are at it, ask them to tell the officer behind us not to shoot when we jump out of the truck," Robin said, motioning towards the back window.

"Will do," Jackson said before the call screen went dark.

Amber glanced in the rearview mirror. "When did we pick him up?"

"When you made the U-turn," Robin replied.

"It's Michigan. U-turns are legal," Amber said, skirting a car that had pulled to the side in front of her.

"Not in the middle of the road in front of a police officer! Besides, at this point, I'm pretty sure he thinks you saw him and ran. I would say this pretty much counts as a police chase!"

Amber bit her bottom lip. "I'm not stopping until I get to McDonald's."

"Don't worry. I'm sure they will let us have visitors in prison."

"You really are the best," Amber said as she swerved around several cars that had pulled to the side to let them pass.

Robin cast a glance over her shoulder. "Hey, Louise, you still want me to tell Dalton you were driving?"

Chapter Nine

Amber turned into the McDonald's parking lot and surveyed the area she'd left only minutes before. Both the space she'd occupied and the one where the minivan had been parked now were filled with different cars. A white Chevy Suburban idled in the space where the minivan was previously parked. "Damn! Well, they couldn't have gone too far. Maybe we should…"

"Maybe we should just stop and see what that officer has to say," Robin said, cutting her off.

"You're right," Amber said, opening the door. She'd no sooner gotten the words out of her mouth when the officer shouted for her to get back in the car.

"What the heck?" Amber said, looking over at Robin.

"I guess Jackson hasn't made the call yet." Robin's normally calm voice was on edge.

"Well, I'll just tell him," Amber said, reaching for the door handle.

"Don't open that door," Robin shouted, grabbing hold of her arm. "Seriously, are you trying to get us shot?"

"Shot?" *Why on earth would they shoot us?*

"Yes, shot." Robin pointed to the officer. "Does he look like he's playing to you?"

Amber turned to look. "What the hell? The guy's got a gun!"

Robin rolled her eyes. "Duh, he's a police officer."

"Yes, but he's pointing it at our car!" Amber said incredulously.

"Yes, I'm pretty sure they do that after all police chases."

"It wasn't a police chase." *I was just trying to find my son.*

"Tell that to him," Robin said.

"Them," Amber corrected as two additional police cars hurried into the lot and angled themselves behind her SUV. A sea of faces were plastered against the windows, staring out. Several customers held cell phones to the glass, obviously snapping photos and recording videos of what was transpiring in the parking lot. Things were really getting out of hand.

"Well shit," Robin complained, "if I'd known you were going to involve us in a police chase, I would have at least put on some lipstick when I went to the bathroom."

"At least you got to go to the bathroom," Amber said, feeling the pressure from her bladder. "Do you think they'll let me go pee before they arrest me?"

"Driver, step out of the vehicle!"

"I guess you are getting ready to find out," Robin replied.

Amber looked over at Robin. "Are you coming?"

"Nope, Louise, you are the driver," Robin said, shaking her head.

Amber let out a worried breath and reached for the door. "I'm coming out. Don't shoot."

"Tell them you're not carrying a gun," Robin offered.

"Good idea. I don't HAVE A GUN!" Amber said, emphasizing having a gun.

"Gun!" someone shouted.

"HOLD YOUR FIRE!" called another equally excited voice. "No gun! No gun!"

"Get down on the ground!"

Amber didn't have to be told twice. She flew to the ground and immediately felt as if she were being crushed. Her mind went to the pregnancy test she'd taken before she left the house. Feeling the weight of the knee on her back, she was grateful it had read negative. The person on top of her was yelling for cuffs. A hand grasped her wrist, yanking her arm behind her back. Instantly, cold steel clamped around her wrist. *Shit!*

"What she'd do?" she heard a voice ask.

"I made a U-turn," Amber whispered in reply.

* * *

Amber paced the floor of the small motel room as she relayed the events of the day to Dalton. "They had already left when we arrived. Jackson arrived before they even let Robin out of the Durango." She cut her eyes to Robin and glared. "He was able to convince the police that I was not a deranged madwoman looking for a cheeseburger fix. They put out an APB on the foster mom and Daxton, giving an updated description of them and the minivan. And, can you believe the cop wrote me a ticket for reckless driving?" Amber said into the phone.

"From what you just told me, you are lucky you weren't arrested," Dalton replied.

"I know. But it really was just a misunderstanding."

"A misunderstanding that could have gotten you killed," he countered.

She knew he was worried and suddenly regretted having told him the details over the phone. "I know."

"Do you want me to come up there?"

Yes.

"No. Everything is under control. Robin and I are in the motel waiting for any word. They have roadblocks set up all over town and along the interstate. They can't have gotten too far."

"Well, if they don't find him by tonight, either you are coming home or I'm driving up."

"Okay," she agreed. "I'll call as soon as I hear something."

"Oh, and I'm canceling my previous comment."

"Which was?"

"I think I'd feel better if you let Robin drive."

"Very funny."

"I just want you home safe, darlin'. I love you."

Amber gripped the phone a little tighter. *I wish you were here.* She still felt on edge and would love nothing more than to have his arms wrapped around her. Funny how a single hug from that man could fix nearly anything. "I love you too."

"Call me if you need me."

I need you. "I will."

"That sounded as if it went well," Robin said as soon as Amber hung up the phone.

"Well as can be expected, considering you almost got me shot."

Robin raised her eyebrows in disbelief. "I almost got you shot?"

"Tell them you don't have a gun," she repeated.

"Yeah. Tell them you don't have a gun. Not, I don't HAVE A GUN!!" Robin said, sounding amazingly like Amber.

Amber laughed. "Yeah, I may have freaked out slightly."

"You think?"

"Yeah, I guess I need to get out more." *Or stay in the house and never leave.*

"Or stay in altogether. It might be safer that way," Robin said, mirroring Amber's thoughts.

Amber rubbed at the red marks on her wrists. "You didn't even get handcuffed."

"No worries. I know what it feels like."

"To be arrested?"

"Handcuffed," Robin said with a wink.

"Brat!" Amber said, tossing a pillow at her and flopping onto the bed closest to her. She rolled over, placing her stomach on the floral comforter, and looked up at her friend. "Do you think they will find them?"

Robin's face turned serious. "I hope so, Chickie. I really do."

* * *

Amber circled the block for the third time, keeping up a brisk pace as she ran. While she wanted to drive around and help with the search, she had been instructed to stay at the motel. Jackson had struck a deal with the police officer: she would not be arrested if she promised to stay out from behind the wheel for the remainder of her stay. They had a room at the Larrimore Inn, the only motel in town. It was family owned and clean, but their double room was small, and the furniture had seen better days. When the walls started closing in on her, Robin had suggested she go for a run. She'd agreed, telling Robin she would be within shouting distance if she heard anything. The inn sat on the corner of a large city block, and Amber decided to contain her route to that one-block circumference. As her feet pounded the pavement, she wondered at the mess she'd made of things. Three and a half years had passed since she'd received the first letter letting her know Heather was in poor health and arrangements might be needed for the child. He'd gone to live with his grandparents shortly after that letter, living with them for the first three years of his life. She'd received the second letter nearly six months ago. Daxton was only three and a half years old, and in that time, he'd lived in three different homes. Three and a half years. The amount of time she'd wasted rejecting the child just because she was pissed off at her dead husband. And why? Was she so angry at Jeff that she couldn't see the gift he'd left behind? *Gift?* How crazy that she now thought of her late husband's love child as a blessing. A shiver went through her as she recalled the horoscope she'd read just before Jeff was killed in the car crash. "Tragedy is a blessing in disguise." At the time, she'd thought that her world had ended. But within days, it was clear that Jeff was not the person she thought him to be. She quickly learned that he'd been cheating the duration of their marriage and that a recent dalliance had produced a love child. Amber's speed increased as she recalled meeting the then-pregnant slut at Jeff's funeral. Heather. She felt her jaw tighten at the thought of the woman who'd shared her husband's bed. A woman he professed to love. A woman for whom he'd planned to leave her. A woman who was now dying of some unknown illness and had turned to Amber for help. The woman must be truly desperate to have even considered asking. The things mothers do for their children. She wondered if she would have been as selfless.

I would do anything for any of my children.

Amber blew out a breath as she turned the corner. *I'm sorry for calling you a slut. But Jeff's still a prick.* Prick or not, if it weren't for Jeff's indiscretions, she and her new husband would not be close to welcoming a new member to their household. She pictured the look of joy on Dalton's face when she'd agreed to adopt Daxton. Her heart fluttered just thinking of the man to whom she was now married. Dalton was going to be a great dad to Daxton. He'd already proven that in the way he'd accepted Julie from the moment they'd first met. And now, after four years of trying, she was finally going to give him a son.

"Thanks, Jeff."

She nearly tripped as the words came out of her mouth. Had she really just said thanks to the man she despised so much? She slowed to a walk, letting her muscles cool down. Yes, she had, and strangely enough, she knew she actually meant it. If it weren't for Jeff's infidelities, there wouldn't be a child. A child she had rejected and who was now being made to dress like a girl, being dragged around by a person who may or may not be mentally unstable. *Of course she is unstable. You saw her yourself. The woman was at the end of her rope.* Amber looked at the cloudless sky.

"Please let us find him."

As she walked past the motel, sweat pouring off her thin frame, her mind turned towards her father. If she could find it in her heart to forgive her ex, shouldn't she be able to forgive the man who, even during his fall from grace, was still more of a father to her than Jeff had ever been to their daughter? Her father had been sober and living under their roof for nearly four years, but Amber still held him at bay, still regarding him as a stranger in her home. Yet never once had the man called her on it. Never had he begged her to forgive him for his neglect. Her heart pounded as a lump formed in her throat. A memory tugged at the edge of her mind, one of her dad trying to explain how her mom was sick and might not be around much longer. She'd pushed him away and refused to listen when he tried to talk to her in those early months as her mother's disease progressed. Little by little, he stopped trying to talk to her and began staying away for longer and longer periods of time. By the time her mother passed, he was deep in the bottle, and Amber was buried so far in her own grief that she had no clue how to reach him. Maybe if she'd tried a little harder, she could have helped pull him from the recesses of the bottle. Maybe if she had listened, he wouldn't have ended up there in the first place. Realizing she was no longer walking, she leaned against the building, swiping at the moisture that poured from her face, only then noticing it was tears that fell and not sweat. She stood against the wall and wept, her heart aching to hold the child she'd never met and to wrap her arms around the man she had pushed away. How could she have made such a mess of things...

Chapter Ten

Amber spent a restless night staring at the clock until nearly three a.m. Only then did she plunge into a deep nightmare-plagued sleep. She was still fighting with unseen demons when the motel phone rang, pulling her from the grips of hell.

"Hello?"

"Amber, did I wake you?"

"Jackson, what time is it?"

"Ten o'clock. Sorry, I thought you'd be awake by now."

Ten? I never sleep this late. "Sorry, I was so stressed out, I didn't get much sleep."

"Well, how about I give you something to smile about?"

Amber shot up in bed, fully awake. "You found him! Where is he? Is he okay? When can I come get him?"

"Whoa. Come on, girl. It's early. One question at a time. We don't have him yet. He's still with his foster mom. But we know where he is. The police are on the way to pick him up as we speak."

"Still with his foster mom! Why? Where? Sorry, just tell me where he is, and I will go get him."

There was silence on the other end. "Jackson?"

"I'm here. Listen, we just have a little issue with turning over custody. The social worker needs to mediate the meeting in neutral surroundings. Then she will decide what is in the boy's best interest."

"Social worker? What social worker? And the boy has a name. It's Daxton and we – me and Dalton – are in his best interest," Amber replied heatedly.

"Now, honey…"

Amber cut him off. "Don't you 'now honey' me. What is this all about?"

"It's just a bit of bureaucratic red tape. It seems like the news got hold of a video with you in handcuffs and now the powers that be just want to make sure that you are fit to raise a child."

Amber jumped off the bed and started pacing the length of the phone cord. "Fit to raise a child! Are you freaking kidding me?!"

"Amber?" the voice on the other end of the phone was eerily calm.

"Yes."

"You are in a motel room, and judging from the outside of the place, the walls are super thin. Could you please keep your voice down? You are not doing anything to help your case."

She blew out a sigh and lowered her voice. "So when will that meeting take place?"

"Much better. I'm not sure. The authorities said they would contact me as soon as they have the child in custody."

"Custody?"

"It's just a figure of speech. The police will call me as soon as they have the boy. Daxton," he amended.

"Why you? You are working for us." Amber knew she was making more of it than she needed to, but she had to lash out at someone, and Jackson was convenient.

"They said they tried to call your cell and your phone went to voicemail."

Amber picked up her phone and stared at the blank screen. *Shit!* "My phone died."

"There now, see? Everything is on the up and up."

"Don't patronize me, Jackson."

"I wouldn't think about it, Amber. I just need you to remain calm and not do anything to draw further attention to yourself. Got it?"

"Got it," she said after a short silence.

"Okay, plug in your phone. Get something to eat and wait for my call."

She waited for him to hang up, then slammed down the receiver. "I am calm!"

The door opened, and Robin entered the room. She held a small bag with her teeth, had two cups of coffee in her left hand, and the motel key in her right. Tossing the key on the dresser, she removed the bag from her mouth. "I brought breakfast."

Amber took one of the cups and tilted it, closing her eyes as the sugary liquid slid down her throat.

"Sheesh, girl, you look like shit. If I hadn't shared a room with you, I'd swear you had gone out drinking last night. You didn't even wake up when I took a shower and got dressed. When did you start snoring?"

Amber was mortified. "I don't snore!"

Robin pulled a doughnut from the bag and offered it to her. "The hell you don't."

Amber felt the tears well in her eyes. *Can this day get any worse?*

Robin flopped in the chair. "Okay, Chickie, out with it."

Amber fought back tears as she relayed her conversation with Jackson.

"Sounds like formalities. I really don't think you have anything to worry about," Robin said when she'd finished.

"That's what Jackson said."

"Well, maybe Dalton will get here in time for the meeting."

"Dalton's coming?"

"Yeah, didn't he call you on the motel phone?"

"Not unless he tried when I was on the line with Jackson. Why did he call you?"

"He got worried when he tried your phone, and it went straight to voicemail."

Amber swiped her phone, and sure enough, she had a voice message from Dalton. "He said he sent me an e-mail."

"And?" Robin asked, peering over her shoulder.

"Hang on. I'm checking." Pulling up the inbox, she clicked on the e-mail he'd sent. Relief washed over her as she read his simple message. "I'm on my way." Fresh tears sprang from her eyes as she clicked on the attachment. The photo showed a clipping from the morning newspaper, her horoscope for the day, which read, "An emotional start to the day could bring a flood of tears." Dalton had placed a handwritten note below the clipping. "If you are going to cry, then I am going to be there to kiss away your tears."

* * *

The meeting was set for two thirty, and thankfully, Dalton arrived in time to hug Amber's jitters away. Not wishing to be in the way, Robin took Amber's Durango and headed for home as soon as Dalton arrived. It was two twenty-five when they pulled open the door of the Larrimore Social Services complex, which housed Judi Haddox's office. The social worker met them at the door. The woman was older than Amber thought she'd be, had short red hair, and a forced smile.

"You must be Mr. and Mrs. Renfro," she said, extending her right hand to Dalton, who removed his cowboy hat and took her hand.

"Dalton Renfro. It's nice to meet you, ma'am," he said with a smile that lit up his face and melted the stern face of the woman he'd focused his attention on. "This pretty lady here is my wife, Amber."

Haddox's face was two shades deeper than it had been when they'd entered the room. Amber smiled, fully aware of the effects of her husband's charms. Charms she knew extended well beyond his boyish face and deep southern drawl.

"Nice to meet you," Amber said, extending her hand.

"Come sit in my office." The woman turned, obviously expecting them to follow. They did, and once inside, Haddox motioned for them to sit. Frames showing various degrees and awards the woman had earned filled one wall. The far wall nearer the desk held what seemed to be personal photos, Haddox and a man, presumably her husband, taken at the beach. Several photos of her standing next to Native American Indians in customary dress, showcasing their heritage. Heritage the woman in front of them didn't seem to share, given her lighter skin coloring. *A powwow, perhaps.* There were several photos of dogs, and numerous ceramic dachshund figurines littered both the desk and adjoining bookshelves. The woman's purse sat on the flat surface behind her desk, a pair of sequined flip-flops protruding out the opening.

"My name is Judi, and I am a flip-flop-oholic," the lady said, seeing where Amber's gaze stopped.

It was Amber's turn to blush. "It just surprised me that you had flip-flops when it is so cool out."

The woman laughed an easy laugh. "Someday I will retire, and when I do, I will move to a location where I can wear flip-flops year round. My job requires me to wear sensible shoes. Unfortunately, the state's idea of sensible and mine are totally different, so I wear them in my office when I'm alone."

Amber looked at Dalton, willing him to ask the obvious question. When he didn't, she took the lead. "Speaking of being alone, where is our son?"

Mrs. Haddox studied her for several seconds before answering. "Daxton is in the meeting room with my receptionist, playing with toys."

Amber felt her heart flutter. *He's here.* "Where?"

"In due time. We have plenty of time for a little chat before I allow you to meet your... son."

It was said as if there was some question as to the truth of the statement. Amber looked at Dalton, whose expression seemed to echo her thoughts.

"Mrs. Haddox," he said before Amber could speak, "exactly what is the problem with us seeing our son?" Dalton asked emphasizing the word "our."

The social worker's lips formed a pucker, then twitched from side to side. She reached for a pair of reading glasses, placed them low on her nose, and plucked a file from the desk. Pulling out several sheets of paper, she looked each of them in the eye and spoke. "It seems as though you are not the only ones laying claim to the boy," she said, thumbing through the papers. Do the names Walt and Connie Wilson mean anything to you?"

Amber felt her chest tighten and anger soared through her veins like bile. "They are my ex-in-laws. What the hell do they want?"

Haddox tilted her head and peered at Amber over her glasses. "So they are indeed the child's grandparents?"

"Only by blood!" Amber said bitterly. "They never wanted anything to do with Julie and they have never even met Daxton."

Haddox lowered the papers to the desk, removed the glasses, and placed them on top of the file. "And you have?"

The words cut through her as if she'd been slapped. No, she hadn't met Daxton. And now she'd made such a mess of things that she might never even get the chance. When she spoke, her words came out in a whisper.

"Not yet. There were extenuating circumstances."

Haddox leaned back in her chair, looking as if she'd just won a strategic game of chess. "As you can see, there are numerous things at play here. The child, Daxton, has been through a great deal in the last few days – years, actually. So I'm sure you will understand why our agency is taking great strides in making sure that the boy is not further traumatized."

"Meaning what?" Dalton inquired.

"Meaning, Mr. Renfro, the child will not be released to you or anyone else," she said, tapping the file, "until I can determine who the key players are."

Dalton leaned forward in his chair. "This is not a game and our son is not a pawn, Mrs. Haddox."

"I am well aware this is not a game. I'm also fully aware that none of the players," she said, using the term once more, "have bothered to come forward in the six months that the child has been in foster care. As I see it, the foster parents are the only ones that stepped up and took care of the child."

"The foster mom kidnapped Daxton and forced him to dress like a girl," Amber replied heatedly.

"And you were involved in a police chase!" Haddox's tone matched hers.

"I was going after MY son!"

"He's not YOUR son!"

"His mother gave him to me," Amber countered.

"You give away a dog. You give away a fish. You do NOT give away a child," the woman spat.

Dalton took hold of Amber's arm before she could reply. "Mrs. Haddox, I'm not sure what you saw on the news or what you've been told, but I assure you your impression of us, of this situation, is all wrong. We may have waited longer than what some would deem appropriate, but we are ready to take responsibility for the boy. Our son," he amended. "We have never even met the child, and we already love him. If it is a fight you want, it is a fight you will get, but I assure you, the law is on our side. Now, are you going to let us see our son or not?"

Chapter Eleven

Amber paced the confines of the small motel room. "This is ridiculous," she said for at least the hundredth time.

While the social worker had agreed to allow them to meet Daxton, when it came time for the meeting, he was asleep. It was decided that instead of waking him, the meeting would be pushed back until morning, something that didn't make sense, since it meant that the child would once again be placed in the care of strangers.

"Since when does social services schedule meetings on Saturdays?"

"Darlin' if you don't calm down, you are going to explode," Dalton said softly.

They'd found out that Jeff's parents, Walt and Connie Wilson, had seen Amber on the news. The reporter had included a brief, unauthorized piece on Amber, and how she was only trying to rescue the child. They'd gone as far to call Daxton a love child with a short but unflattering piece on Amber's late husband, Jeff. Where they'd gotten their info was anyone's guess, but Dalton suspected that to be the motivation for the unexpected turn of events. They'd placed a call to Amber's attorney, Mr. Grether, who was now working the legal angle.

"I can't calm down. Three and a half freaking years without so much as a phone call or visit to Daxton and now they want to be grandparents." Her anger stemmed from much more than that, and they both knew it. While it had been three and a half years for Daxton, they had never reached out to Julie. Any contact was always on Amber's part. She would complain to Jeff, who would say something to his parents just to get Amber off his back. Even though Jeff's parents hated her, she would have welcomed them into Julie's life. Their absence reduced Julie to tears on many occasions, Julie questioning why her grandparents didn't love her. *Seventeen years and nothing, now they are going after Daxton.*

"What's their game?"

Dalton watched as Amber continued to pace her invisible path, nostrils flaring, her black hair trailing behind like a silky mane. Beads of sweat formed at her temples, her eyes wide. He took hold of her toned arm and pulled her into him. She struggled at first, then slowly gave in to his embrace.

"You remind me of a mare in heat. The way they pace in their stalls, waiting for the stallion to come to them."

Amber tossed her head back in laughter. "You did not just say that!"

"See, there you go. Next time, you need to whinny when you do that."

He increased his hold when she attempted to pull away. "Steady there, darlin'. Whoa now," he said, using the voice he reserved for a panicky horse.

Amber giggled. "Dalton Renfro, stop treating me like one of your horses."

He bent his lips to hers and kissed her briefly. He let his mouth graze her jawline before nuzzling her neck in a trail of tender kisses. Turning her around, he lifted her hair, placing it over her shoulder. His hands massaged her tense muscles as his mouth continued its journey along her hairline. She let out a moan and pressed into him.

"You still want me to stop?" The breath of his words blew warmly in her ear, sending shivers down her spine.

She moaned, pressing into him. "I hope this is not how you treat your horses."

"I'll sweet talk them all day and sometimes add a pat on the rear; anything more than that is up to the stallions. If that doesn't work, there is always artificial insemination." The latter was something they'd discussed on a more personal level of late: bringing in a sperm donor to help Amber conceive. They had canceled their appointment after deciding to adopt Daxton. He felt her stiffen and instantly regretted broaching the subject again.

She turned to him, her deep brown eyes blinking back tears. "You wouldn't have said that if you didn't think we had a chance of losing Daxton."

"I will do everything in my power to make sure that doesn't happen. But if it does, we still have other options," he said softly. While the law appeared to be on their side, it wasn't as cut and dried as he'd hoped. The fact that the social worker hadn't relented right away had Dalton more than a little concerned.

Tears pooled in her eyes. He pulled her into him and held her as she sobbed.

"It's going to be okay, darlin'. It's all going to be okay," he repeated, praying it was true.

Her sobs softened, her breathing returning to normal. Dalton lessened his grip. Amber peered up at him, her face still glistening with the recent tears. "I need you."

"Now?" It wasn't that he didn't want to.

"I need to know that I haven't screwed up everything in my life."

"Amber, you haven't...this is not your fault" He stopped when she lifted her fingers to his lips to silence his lies. He led her to the edge of the bed and waited as she stripped from her clothes and scrambled on top of the flowery comforter. He watched as the goosebumps rose on her naked body, her flesh quivering even though the room was warm. He removed his clothes and climbed onto the bed. His body responded to her need as he felt her trembling beneath him. Placing his hands on the bed, he pushed away. Wanting more, he moved to taste her juices.

She shook her head, pulling him back.

"I'm ready. I just need to feel you inside of me," she said, opening her legs to him.

He pushed into her, feeling her warmth embrace him. He rose and plunged again, going deeper this time, and continued as she met him with every stroke. They'd made love countless times, but this time felt different. Each time he sank into her, he pushed a little harder and yet it felt as if she needed more. As if she wanted him to punish her for all she thought she'd done. She didn't say a word – didn't have to; her eyes said it all. Staring at him, begging him to take her guilt away. He took hold of her wrists, raised her arms above her head, and continued his assault. He held off as long as he could until he finally exploded inside her in one last punishing push. When drained, he collapsed on the bed beside her, recovering as he waited for her to speak.

"I needed that," she said at last. "Thank you for making love to me."

"That wasn't making love," he said, choosing his words carefully. "You wanted me to hurt you."

"You didn't," she said at last.

He rolled onto his side, brushing the hair aside so he could look into her eyes. "Why?"

"You wouldn't understand," she said, closing her eyes.

"Then make me understand."

She opened her eyes, staring at him for several seconds before speaking. "I just feel like I keep making a huge mess of things."

"What things, Amber?"

"Life."

He sighed. "You act as if you are the only one who has ever made a bad decision."

"I've made more than my share of them," she said and went on to tell him of her recent memories of pushing her dad away, and of the guilt of pushing him into the bottle.

"You did not put that bottle in his hand, Amber."

"I may as well have."

"Bullshit!" Dalton was not normally one to use profanity, but he was frustrated beyond words. "I'm sorry. I am just so tired of you beating yourself up all the time. You were just a child when your mom died. You are no more to blame for her getting sick than you are for your dad becoming an alcoholic. He has a disease, just like your mom had a disease. You say you pushed him into it? Well, he should have pushed back. You were just a little girl, Amber. It wasn't up to you to make the rules. It was up to him. If your child tries to push you away, you pull them closer. Hug them even tighter. It's what parents do. They don't leave you to run the streets and get knocked up by the first man who pays attention to you." Dalton froze, realizing he had just crossed the line.

When Amber tried to scramble from the bed, he held her tight. "I'm sorry. I shouldn't have said that."

"Why not? It's true," she said coldly.

"Amber, it is true, but the way I said it was harsh. I'm pissed off. Pissed at the crappy hand you've been dealt. Pissed that I wasn't the one that found you from the beginning so that all the bad things in your life had never happened to you. Pissed that I can't produce enough sperm to give you the baby you desperately want. I was not with you yesterday. I wonder if maybe, just maybe, I would have recognized Daxton from the photograph and would have stopped the events that have unfolded since then."

"Oh, Dalton, you can't blame yourself for any of that," Amber said, turning to him.

"Why not?"

"Because none of it is your fault. If you had been there from the beginning, you wouldn't have Katie Mae, and I wouldn't have Julie."

"Exactly! Can't you see you have been carrying this load around like a bag of sand? It is weighing you down and trying to steal away our happiness. The day we got married was one of the happiest days of my life. I thought, here is a woman I can spend the rest of my life with. A woman who will put the joy back into my life. You have been so tied up in guilt that it is eating you alive and stealing the joy from you and those around you. You have to stop living in the past and start enjoying the love that is all around us. We have Julie, Katie Mae, and family. Lots of family, Amber. Soon we WILL have our son. I promise you that. I will not allow Connie, Walt, or any damn social worker take that boy away from us. He needs us as much as we need him. Promise me that from this day forward, you will focus on the positive and not worry about things, real or imagined, that you have no power to change."

"I promise." Her words came out in a whisper.

"I love you, Amber. I want nothing more than to make you happy and to never give you a reason to cry again. But you have to meet me halfway. Promise!"

"I promise," she said with meaning. She made a move to rise, and he pulled her back to him.

"Not so fast, darlin'." He straddled her, kissing her forehead, then pressed off and worked his way down her body in slow, deliberate kisses.

"Where are you going?" she questioned.

"We did it your way last time. Now we are going to do it mine." He lowered his head and breathed in the smell of them. He might not be able to control a lot of things, but at least for tonight, he could fill her with everything he had. Tonight, he could make her feel loved.

Chapter Twelve

Amber woke more relaxed than she'd felt in a long time. It was as if a weight she didn't know she was carrying suddenly lifted from her shoulders. Stretching, she rolled over to find the bed empty. She reached for the note draped across Dalton's pillow.

Darlin, you were sleeping so soundly I didn't want to wake you. Went to the store, I'll be back soon. Love Dalton. PS, you are cute when you snore!

"I do not snore!" Amber crumpled the note and threw it at the wall. She stuck her bottom lip out in a pout, angry that her relaxed mood had been compromised. It was cold in the room, or perhaps it was the fact that she wasn't wearing any clothes.

The door opened, and an icy chill ran through her as Dalton came in carrying two coffees and a paper bag. Great, just what her waistline needed, more doughnuts. She was already bloated from all the fast food she'd eaten since leaving home.

I'm going to turn into a fat-snoring-old lady.

"Good morning, beautiful," he said before she could voice a protest.

"Mr. Renfro," she said, narrowing her eyes and pulling the covers higher.

His brows went up in question. For a moment, she thought he was going to go back out the same door he'd just entered.

"I don't snore," she said when at last he took a step.

"*Au contraire*, milady," he said, placing his bounty on the dresser. "You don't rattle the rooftops by any means, but you do indeed snore."

"Why didn't you tell me?" Not that she could do anything about it, but at least she'd have known.

"I thought you knew."

"How would I know what I do when I sleep?"

A sly smile crossed his face.

"What?" Amber asked, suddenly afraid of what other bodily functions she might be guilty of.

"I guess you don't know about the other thing."

Oh God, There's more? "What other thing?"

"You talk in your sleep," he said with a sly grin.

She crossed her arms. When she did, the blanket slid down, nearly exposing her bare breasts. "Do not."

"Oh, you most assuredly do," he said, staring at her bosom. "You mumble little incoherent sentences. And, sometimes you moan in your sleep."

"If you are referring to last night, I was not sleeping."

In fact, neither of them had slept very much last night. Dalton had seen to that. The man was practically insatiable.

"No, last night, you were fully awake," he said, his eyes twinkling as he recalled the events of the previous night.

"Don't even think about it," she warned.

"I wouldn't dream of it," he said, moving closer.

She backed away from him. "This is not a good idea. I can barely walk as it is."

"Happy to kiss it and make it all better," he said, unbuttoning his shirt.

He removed his pants, and Amber pulled the covers higher.

"I'm serious, Dalton. You stay away from me."

He tossed his briefs to the floor, took hold of the covers, and pulled them off with a single whip of the hand. His icy grip covered her foot, sending an instant chill throughout her body. He smiled, tickling the insole when she tried to pull away. Grabbing the other foot, he pulled her towards him. She tried to wiggle from his grasp, twisted, and ended up on her stomach.

"Oh, so this is the way it's going to be." His voice was low and dangerously lust-filled.

She felt the bed move under his added weight. Before she could answer, cold hands cupped her cheeks, gently massaging the roundness of her ass. She made a move to escape as his hands pressed against her flesh, then moved between her legs, gently gliding in circles before dipping into her depths. She felt her body respond and let out a moan as his fingers found what they were seeking. She pushed against him, surprised at how ready she was to pick up where they'd left off only a few hours before. Disappointment washed over her when his fingers discontinued their dance. Her disappointment was short lived as he lowered himself on top of her. Just as the heaviness became too much, he lifted to relieve her of his full weight. He slid between her legs without entering, rocking back and forth in the slick essence his fingers had left behind. She pushed back with every stroke, waiting in anxious frustration for him to finally take the plunge. Her need grew as he continued to tease her with his hardness. Each time he tilted forward, she thought he would enter, but each pass met with disappointment. He was toying with her, waiting for her to beg.

I can't hold out much longer.

"Okay. I give. Stop teasing me," she finally cried as he rejected her once more. Her frustration ebbed when he finally filled her confines, probing deep within her warmth before pulling back in long, deliberate strokes. It didn't take long before they both moaned their release, rocking in unified contentedness. Seconds later, she felt his weight on top of her, his breath coming in rapid bursts just beside her ear.

"Still sore?" he asked as he rolled off of her.

"I may never walk again," she said with a satisfied sigh.

* * *

"Why on earth are we stopping here?" Amber asked as Dalton turned in to the farm supply parking lot.

"Ammunition," Dalton replied.

"Excuse me?"

"Just leveling the playing field. I'll be right back." He put the truck into park and got out before she could respond.

Amber's phone rang. "Hello?"

"You sound worried," Robin said when she answered.

"Does Tractor Supply sell ammo?" Amber asked.

"Not that I know of. Should I be worried?"

"Not as long as you are right," Amber said, staring out the window. "Did you make it home okay?"

"Yeah, ran into a bit of construction, but nothing major. How are things there? When are you bringing the kid home?"

Amber blew out a sigh. "We are on our way to meet him."

"Meet him? What have you been doing since I left?"

"Enjoying our alone time," Amber said, adjusting her position in the seat.

"Okay, now I'm really confused. How much alone time can you have with a toddler running around?"

"That's just it, we don't have a kid running around," Amber replied. "Seems like Connie and Walt saw me on the news and have suddenly decided to file for custody."

"Are you freaking kidding me?"

"I wish I was," Amber said with a sigh.

"What the frick? Since when are they interested in being grandparents?"

"I don't think they are," Amber said, praying it was true.

"Yet they are trying to get custody?"

"Mr. Grether thinks they are just trying to make waves. Just slowing things up to hurt me."

"Yeah, that sounds like something they would do."

"She, not they. Walt has always been a yes man. I'm pretty sure this is all Connie's doing."

"Agreed. Sounds like something the bitch would do. Want me to come back up there and kick her ass?"

Amber laughed into the phone. "I'll let you know."

"You seem to be taking this pretty well."

Another laugh. "I've already had my meltdown. Besides, I'm too tired to be angry."

"Didn't sleep well? Maybe you should cut back on the caffeine."

Amber looked at the cup she still held in her hand. "I don't think it was the coffee."

"Oh?"

"No," Amber said, smiling.

"Ohhhh."

"Yeah," Amber said, knowing her friend had reached the right conclusion.

"All night?"

"All night," Amber said, glancing towards the building. *What on earth is taking so long?*

"Let me get this straight. You almost get arrested, are told the demons from hell are fighting you on custody of the child you are supposed to adopt, and oh, you ended up on the evening news. What on earth could the man have said to have gotten you in the mood?" Robin asked, sounding surprised.

Amber laughed.

"Oh, it must be good."

Another laugh.

"Okay, out with it."

The door to the building slid open, and Dalton came out holding two bags. *Shit, he really did buy ammo.* "Not now, girlfriend. Dalton is coming."

"AMBER! Don't you dare hang up that phone without telling me," Robin yelled.

"He called me a horse," Amber said, laughing.

"And that's your idea of romantic?"

"No, but it worked for Dalton," she said, hanging up the phone.

"What took so long?" Amber asked as Dalton slid behind the wheel.

"Took me a bit to find what I was looking for," he said, buckling his seatbelt.

"You didn't really buy ammo, did you?"

"Not the kind you're thinking of," he said, handing her one of the bags. He dropped the second bag on the seat behind them.

Opening the bag he'd handed her, Amber reached inside and brought out a small horse about five inches tall. Jet black, it posed a striking resemblance to Dalton's horse. Next was a black and white horse with similar markings to Amber's horse. She smiled, remembering the day Dalton had given her the mare. They had known each other for a very short time but had already fallen in love. Amber had told Dalton about the paint horse she'd ridden as a child. She told him that her mother had led her around while she rode the painted mare and wished her mother was there. She ended the conversation, saying it was wishful thinking. The warm memory of her mother had apparently stuck with him. He'd found a horse much like the one in her memories and gifted it to her, naming the horse Wishful Thinking, Wish for short.

"It looks like Wish."

"No crying," Dalton said, keeping his eyes on the wheel.

Next out of the bag was a palomino. Amber stroked the white mane of the yellow plastic horse that represented Katie's horse before digging into the bag and bringing out another black horse. This one had white stockings and a white muzzle.

Julie's horse.

She reached into the bag and removed the last horse.

"An appaloosa?" she asked, holding up the spotted horse.

"Good job," he said, brimming.

"I've had a good teacher." She turned the horse in her hands. It was beautiful, whitish-grey with dark mane and stockings, and equally dark spots upon its rump. "Daxton?"

"It was crazy." Excitement filled Dalton's voice. "I was going to get a tractor, and then I saw the display of horses. When I looked, I was surprised to find one that matched each of our horses. I was getting ready to check out when I realized I hadn't gotten one for Dax. So I asked the saleslady. When I told her why, she went to the back to see if she could find another horse and that is what she found. That's what took so long."

"You are an amazing man, Mr. Renfro," she said, swelling with love.

"The last time you called me that, you didn't sound as impressed."

"The last time you called me a horse."

"I said you reminded me of a mare in heat. Big difference. And to be fair, I think it was before I called you a horse. You were mad because I said you snore."

"I do not snore. And a mare is still a horse," she said with a pout.

"Yes, but I like horses," he said with a wink.

Chapter Thirteen

They arrived ninety minutes before their ten-thirty appointment time in hopes of seeing Daxton sooner. The sign on the door stated business hours to be between nine a.m. and four p.m., Monday - Friday. Dalton held the door for Amber and followed her into the building. They crossed through the empty waiting room to get to the reception area. The receptionist looked up as they approached the glass. She stood to greet them, glanced down at the schedule, to a door marked "meeting room," and back to them. Obviously, they'd caught her unaware.

Don't even think of asking us to come back, Amber thought as the girl slid open the window.

"Mr. and Mrs. Renfro? You are early," she said hesitantly.

The girl, who looked younger than Julie, seemed much too young to be working as a receptionist in any business, much less one who would be the first line of defense between an angry parent and their social worker. Still, she was dressed the part, wearing business casual. Her auburn hair was tucked into a tidy bun. She wore glasses that hid her face and a name tag that stated her name to be Racheal.

"Just a little," Amber replied, trying her best to keep her voice pleasant. When Racheal didn't immediately offer, Amber added, "We were hoping that maybe we could get to see Daxton early."

Racheal slid another uneasy glance towards a closed door. "I'm sorry. Your appointment is not until ten thirty."

"Yes, I know we are early, but we are just so very excited to meet our son," Amber said, forcing a smile.

"I understand, but your appointment is not for another hour and a half. Maybe you could go to breakfast and come back?" Racheal suggested.

"Oh, we've already had breakfast," Amber informed her. She was trying hard to stay calm, something she found increasingly difficult to do.

Dalton moved up beside Amber, removed his hat, and slid a hand through the length of his hair. When he spoke, his words slid out of his mouth like soft butter on a hot roll.

"Well, darlin', if the boy is here...and we are here, it sure would be mighty nice of you if we could move that time up a wee bit."

Racheal's face turned crimson as Dalton's southern charm took hold. She lowered her eyes and rifled through a pile of papers on her desk until she regained her composure. "He is, but... he's... well, he is busy at the moment."

Something was terribly wrong. Amber could feel it in the pit of her stomach. She looked towards the closed door that seemed to be the only obstacle between them and their son.

"Busy how? He's three years old. It's not like he could be in a meeting," Amber challenged.

Racheal returned to her seat. "I'm not at liberty to say."

"Not at liberty to say? He's three years old," Amber repeated, feeling the heat rising in her face. "You need to get Mrs. Haddox on the phone and have her come out here and explain to us what is going on with our son. If you don't, I'm going to go and find out for myself."

"My wife's just anxious to meet our son," Dalton said, taking hold of Amber's arm. "We will be sitting right out here."

He escorted Amber to the waiting area, motioning for her to sit and taking the seat beside her. "Amber Mae, I know you are anxious to see Dax. So am I. Remember what happened yesterday? They could tie this thing up for weeks with a swipe of the pen."

"What kind of games are they playing? Why all the secrecy? What kind of meeting?" Amber asked.

"I don't know, but I intend to ask as soon as Mrs. Haddox comes out," Dalton assured her.

"You have to beat me to it," Amber grumbled.

She pulled out her cell phone and checked to make sure it had power. She watched as Racheal shut the glass window, picked up the phone, turned her back to them. No doubt calling to say they were here.

"I'm so over all of this red tape. Why hasn't Mr. Grether returned my call?"

Dalton placed an arm around her shoulders. "He said he would call as soon as he hears something. It's barely past nine on a Saturday morning. To tell you the truth, I'm not all that sure we will hear anything until Monday. Look around; this place is deserted. It is not even a normal workday. We are lucky to have this appointment. "

Amber blew out a sigh. "I hate that you are always so calm."

"No you don't," he said with a chuckle.

"No I don't," she agreed. "But how can you stay calm with all that is going on?"

"Would you prefer I kick open the door, lasso the kid, and make a break for it?"

"And if I said yes?"

"I'd have to go back to the farm store to get some rope. By the time I drive to the store, buy the rope, and get back, it will be time to see our son."

"Always the voice of reason. What kind of meeting?" she asked once more.

"Probably watching television."

"You think so?" She didn't, but it would calm her nerves if he said yes.

It was Dalton's turn to sigh. "No, the receptionist is too nervous."

"The receptionist is in over her head. She is way too young to be in this line of work." Amber said, glancing at the glass enclosure.

"She did her job," he reminded her.

Amber sat, legs crossed, bouncing the top leg. Finally, she uncrossed her legs and stood. "I can't just sit here. I'm going for a walk."

"Remember what I said about not causing trouble," he warned.

"I remember."

Amber paced the room. She walked closer to the reception desk, hoping to hear what was being said, but only heard muted warbling from the other side of the glass. She moved to the wall of magazines just next to the door marked "meeting room," pretending to read the covers. She gathered up a magazine, moved closer to the door, and thumbed through the pages. She leaned closer to the door, straining to hear something on the other side. Once again, she heard nothing. She ached to open the door and barge inside. Meeting Dalton's gaze, she reconsidered. He was right; doing so would only make things worse. She fought the urge to once again blame herself for the mess she'd created. Dalton was keeping a close eye on her. She smiled at him, then returned the magazine to the rack, snatched up a book, and thumbed through it before returning it to the same spot. Frustrated, she moved to the front window, staring mindlessly out into the parking lot. She conjured up an image of Daxton, wondering what it was going to be like to actually see him in person and wondering what he would think of them. He had been through a lot in his young life, but children were resilient, and they would be able to offer him stability. Would he like them? She didn't have any doubts about Dalton's ability to win the child over but was still feeling insecure about her own abilities.

You'll find out soon enough.

As her mind started to relax, she began to focus on the vehicles in the front lot. There were two. Dalton's big Dodge 3500 pickup truck up near the front of the building and an older car backed into a space at the far end of the lot. *Not a worker*. She knew from yesterday's visit that they had designated parking at the back of the building. She turned, scanning the waiting room once more before focusing her attention on the car.

A meeting with whom?

She didn't recognize the car at first. Why would she? It had been over four years since she'd seen it. But as soon as she did, there was no doubt it was the same vehicle. The one she'd last seen leaving her driveway at a high rate of speed. The one belonging to her ex-in-laws. Connie and Walt were here. In the back, meeting with her son. Her heart thumped in her chest as she forced her voice to remain calm.

"Dalton. Can you come over here, please?"

He was by her side in an instant, his face crinkled with worry. "What is it, darlin'?"

"That's Walt and Connie's car," she said, pointing her chin.

He stiffened beside her. "Are you certain?"

She closed her eyes, remembering the last time she'd seen the car. It was the evening of Jeff's funeral. She had just learned that Walt and Connie had not only known of Jeff's infidelities but had tried to talk him out of a relationship with Heather. They were upset that once again he'd gotten someone they didn't approve of pregnant. It was the first time in the length of her marriage that she'd stood up to her in-laws, reminding them that their precious son was in no way the perfect human being they'd made him out to be. Incensed that she'd dared speak to them that way, they'd stormed out, nearly leaving Jeff's sister, Dianna, behind. *Dianna.* In all the chaos, she'd forgotten all about Jeff's sister. While she hadn't spoken to the woman since that day, they had once been friends. She couldn't help think that Dianna would be on her side.

I wonder what she would have to say about all of this.

Amber looked at the beige Chrysler parked under a tree at the far end of the lot. Why hadn't they pulled to the front of the building? Why did they feel the need to hide their presence? The knot in her stomach tightened. A burning hole of nauseous bile threatened to rise in her throat. She swallowed it down and shook her head.

"It's been a while, but yes, I'm sure it's them."

Chapter Fourteen

How either of them had had the presence to walk outside and make a phone call instead of bursting through the closed door to retrieve Daxton was still a mystery, but they had done that very thing. Dalton leaned against the outside of the building, watching as Amber paced the parking lot, phone plastered to her ear, heatedly relating the latest developments to her attorney, John Grether. The morning air was crisp, but Amber seemed not to notice as she waved her free hand through the air. Her breath came out in foggy wisps of Michigan air as she spoke. Amber always regarded Dalton as the calm one, but in reality, at this very moment, he was ready to explode. He understood it was the social worker's job to go through legal channels to see to the best interest of the child. He commended her for that. However, to keep both him and Amber away while those people were allowed in, that crossed a line. What made them think that Jeff's parents were in any way the best people to raise his son? And Daxton was his son. Maybe not by flesh and blood, but he fell in love with the boy the second he held his photo and saw those bright green eyes staring back at him. Dalton blew out a cloud of breath and shoved his hands into his pocket to keep from slamming his fist into the wall. The law was on their side, and he knew it. This was all legal bullshit. That was the problem. Amber had dealt with enough BS for a lifetime. Why this? Why now? Just when it seemed as if he'd nearly gotten her to stop blaming herself for things that weren't her fault.

Amber had stopped and was apparently listening to the voice on the other end of the phone. She pushed the hair away from her face, showing the flame in her cheeks. Whatever the man was saying, it didn't look as if his little filly approved. He knew in his heart she was once again blaming herself for the mess she'd made. If only she'd trusted him enough to have come to him earlier, then maybe this could have all been avoided. He didn't see that lack of trust as a reflection on their current relationship but instead a carryover from what her previous husband had put her through.

Pulling his hands from his pocket, he balled them into fists. Not for the first time since meeting Amber, Dalton wished that her late husband were still alive. What he wouldn't give to be able to punch Jeff right in the nose. The man had caused Amber so much grief. Grief that continued, even though he was long dead and buried. Like a lot of exes, the man had lied, cheated, and tried to steal everything, his ultimate goal to leave Amber with a huge debt that she had no means of repaying. If he hadn't been killed in the accident, he would have succeeded. Right after his death, a distraught Amber had turned everything over to her attorney to sort out. It was the attorney who'd discovered Jeff had cleaned out their savings account and forged Amber's name in an attempt to remortgage their house the week before his accident. If not for Grether, Amber would have been caught up in a legal nightmare. Grether was a good attorney; no doubt he would fix their current situation just as he had when Jeff died. Dalton pulled up an image of the man from a photo he'd seen. The guy was dressed to perfection, had spiky blonde hair and a smile that belied what a lying, cheating snake he really was. The man had to learn those traits from someone. Now the most obvious someones were inside that building, all nice and warm, filling the head of both the social worker and that innocent child with who knew what. The image of Jeff's parents soiling Daxton with their lies infuriated him. Enough was enough. Dalton tucked his fists into his armpits, pushed off the building, and moved towards the door. He stopped after only a few steps, staring at his reflection in the mirror. While his attire might give him the appearance of a rough and tumble cowboy, he was, in reality, a true southern gentleman. He'd never hit anyone in anger, and he wasn't going to start now. He had to let things play out and pray the legal system would do its job. As he stared in through the glass, the door to the meeting room opened, and a man more than double his age stepped out. Dalton felt the tension in his arms wane.

Great, you were going to pummel an old man.

The man stopped once clear of the doorframe and waited as a woman who looked to be of similar age appeared in the doorway. The woman's face was strained and unsmiling. The man's curved appearance showed he'd long since used up his best years. The couple turned to face the door they'd just exited. Dalton's breath caught as he saw a small figure appear in the same doorway.

Daxton.

The woman reached her arms to the child, quickly lowering them again as the boy disappeared from view. Rejected, the woman pulled away from her husband, who reached a hand to her arm. A scowl appeared on her face as she further shrugged off her husband's attempt at comfort. The man shook his head, turned, and followed the child back into the room. The woman started to follow him, but the door was closed in her face. The rage on her face as she sat in a nearby chair gave him pause.

Dalton removed his cowboy hat, ran a hand through his hair, then returned the hat to his head. These were not people to hate. These were people to pity. He turned towards Amber, his anger forgotten.

* * *

Amber ended the call just as Dalton approached. The set of his shoulders and smiling face showed a man who didn't seem to have a care in the world. She envied his ability to remain calm in situations where she wanted to run and scream. It was that very calmness that kept her from coming unhinged.

Her phone rang. "Yes," she said, answering Julie's call.

"Hi, Mom, what's up? Got anything you want to tell me?" her daughter's voice called through the receiver.

"No. Things are a bit crazy at the moment. If this is not an emergency, we can talk later. Okay?"

"Sure, no problem," Julie said, ending the call.

"Anything new?" Dalton asked as he neared.

"That was Julie. She sounded a bit short. Obviously, she is still on edge about being left behind. I'll make it up to her when we get home. Mr. Grether just keeps telling me not to worry, assuring me that we have the law on our side."

"We may have more than that," Dalton said.

"What?"

"I just saw the Wilsons," he said, glancing over his shoulder. "They are old."

"Not really." Amber thought back to the last time she'd seen Jeff's mom. It was just after the funeral. She was stylish but looked haggard. At the time, she'd just thought it was the weight of losing a son. But looking back, she did seem older than she remembered. "Maybe."

"No maybes, darlin'. Those people are old."

"Okay, so they are old. I don't understand…"

Dalton cut her off before she could finish. "Because no judge in their right mind is going to award them custody over us. Not that it will get that far."

Amber felt her body relax. "That is pretty much what Mr. Grether just said."

"What else did he say?"

"He feels confident this is just a pissing contest. His words," she added when she saw Dalton's brows go up. "I think he is right. But my gut tells me that Connie is the one spearheading this. Walt doesn't say boo without her permission."

Dalton's eyes took on a dangerous gleam. "You are sexy when you get riled up."

She took a step back. "The last time you looked at me like that, you called me a horse."

He laughed. "I said you reminded me of a mare in heat."

He took a step closer and pulled her into him, kissing her briefly before releasing her. "And that was behind closed doors. Today, we have more important things to do."

"So now we wait for them to leave," she said reluctantly.

"No, darlin', now we storm the castle."

"Mr. Grether told me we should not confront them," Amber said when he took her hand and started for the building. "He made me promise to play nice."

Dalton turned and flashed his boyish grin. "Darlin', I always play nice."

Chapter Fifteen

One hour earlier…

Judi Haddox took a breath to steady herself. The chance she was taking would be a career ender if not for one thing. Judi was already technically retired. She'd even had a retirement ceremony and was only here because her replacement ended up having an emergency appendectomy a week before she was due to take over. So in essence, Judi herself was now a fill-in and technically untouchable. Her belongings were already tucked inside boxes in the corner, waiting to be carried out for the very last time. Upon agreeing to stay, she had retrieved a few personal things from the boxes, rehung her certificates, along with a few photos to make the drab office more bearable. She was taking a chance bringing in the two families during non-business hours. She'd even brought in her niece to keep up normal appearances; just another day in the child services office. Only it wasn't just another day. It was Saturday, and a decision needed to be made. If she left this until next week, the boy would end up in another foster care home until custodianship was determined and that could take months.

She leafed through the file on her desk and stopped to look at the photos in front of her. She placed them in two stacks, each one representing the parties involved. Most of them were taken from the Internet the evening before. Google was a mighty handy tool, especially when one was limited to very few hours to compose a history. Since her replacement was due to start on Monday, that was exactly what Judi had, a few hours. She picked up the first photo and turned it over to read the names, Walter and Connie Wilson. Older – probably late sixties to early seventies. Well dressed and presumably pillars of their community. Their age nagged at her. Provided they lived, they would each be in their late eighties to early nineties when the child graduated high school. If they died early, the boy could revert to foster care as a teen, and that was too horrible to imagine. With few people willing to adopt teenagers, most teens spent their youths hopping from one foster home to another. Still, as grandparents, they had a legitimate claim to the child. *Then why wait until now? The child is three years old. Why only after the former daughter-in-law decides to adopt the child are they suddenly interested? Maybe they saw Amber's photo on the news and are truly concerned about the child's safety.*

She pictured the woman she'd met the previous day. Amber seemed a bit emotional, but nothing that raised any flags. Judi rifled through the second pile and pulled out a picture of Amber. *Pretty. Almost has a Sandra Bullock thing working. But tell me, can you really love a child fathered by your late husband?*

She already does.

The thought came as if whispered in her ear. Judi sifted through the photos and found a photo of two girls. It had taken some doing, but she'd found the photo and several more of the family on the website of a photography studio in Lexington, Kentucky. She studied the girls. The two looked nothing alike, yet they were smiling and regarding the other like they'd known each other all their lives. The older girl had green eyes and brown hair, and the younger girl sported jet black hair with blue eyes. *The stepdaughter looks more like Amber than her own daughter.* Judi was just about to return the photo to the pile when another thought hit her. *Julie and the boy share the same father.* She compared the photo with the one she had of the boy and easily saw the resemblance.

She picked up the first photo once more. *So if you two are so eager to be grandparents, then why were you not there for your first grandchild? Why now?* she questioned once more. *Why choose one grandchild over the other? Because it was a boy?* She didn't think so. If that were the reason, they would have come forward before now. She kept that photo and held the picture of Amber beside it, looking from one to the other. *Do you really give a shit about the child or are you only doing this to spite the ex-wife?*

It's right in front of you, Judi. Don't send that child into a loveless home.

She set the photos aside and continued. The next photo was of Dalton's house. She'd found this photo and multiple others in an online copy of an equestrian magazine. The magazine did a story on Dalton Renfro, telling of his many accomplishments in the horse community. According to the article, Mr. Renfro had started with nothing and was now one of the largest horse breeders in Lexington, Kentucky. Several of his horses had impressive records, and two had run in the Kentucky Derby, one placing very well.

So the guy has money, and he's good-looking. That doesn't make him a good dad.

She focused on the photograph, studying it as if she were a detective looking at a crime scene. *Come on, tell me your secrets.* To say the house was impressive would be an understatement. A stately, two-story southern mansion, complete with columns and a huge wraparound porch. She smiled. The house reminded her of something out of the movie *Gone with the Wind.* She picked up a second photo, which looked as if it was taken from an airplane. It showed the same house from above, along with multiple horse barns and miles and miles of wooden fencing.

Any child would thrive in those surroundings.

She set the photos aside with a frustrated sigh. *This case should be cut and dried. The mother has repeatedly expressed her desire to have the child given to her boyfriend – dead boyfriend,* she corrected herself. *Dead boyfriend's wife. Who does that? Okay, she's dying. But why not offer the child to the husband's parents? It's not like either the wife or the grandparents have ever seen the child. She hates the mother. So why would you offer your child to someone you hate? To make her miserable?* Judi rubbed her temples. *What am I missing here?* She flipped through the papers once more, pulling out an affidavit she'd somehow overlooked. *So the wife set*

up a trust fund for her late husband's love child. You're
more of a woman than I am, Amber Renfro. Judi picked
up the photo of the grandparents. *Is that it? Do you
need money? Do you hope to get your hands on the kid's
trust fund? Maybe.* She put the photo down. *Okay, so
the trust fund could be the answer to why the Wilsons
want the child, but why does the mother not want the
parents to have him? Maybe it was something the father
told her. What could be so bad that it would keep her from
granting them custody? Maybe they were abusive...* A
knock on the door brought her from her musings.

"Yes?"

The door opened, and Racheal peeked in. "Mr.
and Mrs. Wilson have arrived for their
appointment."

Judi looked at her niece, who had agreed to act
as the secretary for the weekend. "How's the boy?"

"Daxton is adorable. We've been coloring in
the meeting room. Now he's playing with the train
station."

"Okay, give me five minutes to get situated,
then you can show them in," she said, picking up the
contents on her desk and returning them to the file.

Racheal hesitated. "Are you going to get in
trouble for this?"

Judi pushed back from the desk. "How do you
mean?"

"Mom thinks you are up to something. She
said you need to let the court decide who gets
custody."

"Ultimately, they will. I just want to make sure
the boy is going to the right place."

Again, the girl hesitated. "What place is that?"

"The place where he will ultimately call his home." *If only it were that simple.*

Racheal frowned. "And if you pick the wrong place?"

"Honey, I've been doing this for twenty-four years. My files are full of children who've been pulled in different directions and ultimately ended up in juvie. I've made good decisions and bad, and for each bad decision, there is a price to pay. The decisions made in this building can make or break a child. Or, it can set up a chain of events that not only ruins the life of the child but of the child's children as well. This is my one last chance to get it right." She turned to the desk, picked up a photo of Daxton, and held it up for her niece to see. "This little man is only three years old. In the three years he's been alive, he has lived in three different homes. That's not counting the last two nights spent with us."

She'd gone out on a limb with that one, but she was not about to turn him over to another foster home after what he'd just been through.

"He needs a home where he can feel safe. He needs parents that will be there for him, kiss his boo-boos, correct him when he's wrong, and praise him when he does well. And, he needs to go to the home today. If I don't place him, then he will go back into foster care and be bumped around until everything is settled. He needs a win." *I need a win.*

Racheal looked at her in awe. "I didn't know your job was so difficult."

Judi shrugged. "It has its rewards."

"Do you know who you are going to pick?"

"I know the logical choice," Judi said with a sigh.

"If you've made up your mind, why set up the meetings?"

Why indeed. "There are pieces to the puzzle I still can't figure out."

"So you bring them all in, give them a hard time, and see who breaks? Why, Aunt Judi, you're a modern-day Willy Wonka." Racheal laughed.

"Only instead of a golden ticket, we have a golden-haired child." Judi glanced at the photo in her hand. "Time to put my bitch face on."

"You wear it so well." Racheal giggled. She gave her aunt a quick hug before leaving.

Judi returned the photo to the desk, opened her desk drawer, and pulled out a different photo. The photo showed a battle scene of Native Americans on the Great Plains facing off with soldiers. Closing her eyes, she whispered a prayer. "Oh, great spirit whose voice I hear in the winds. Hear me. I am small and weak. I need your strength. Guide me and give me the wisdom to decide what is best for this child. Give me a sign so that I will know beyond a shadow of doubt and let the breaths of my ancestors whisper to me the answer." Judi glanced at the photo on her desk. She was not Native American, but she'd heard a similar poem a few years ago during an Indian powwow, and it resonated with her. Maybe she was crazy, but she'd used the poem on multiple occasions, and it seemed to work. With one last glance at the picture, she gathered her courage and left to face her own battle.

Chapter Sixteen

Dalton held the door for Amber. Connie looked up when they entered, and the temperature in the room dropped twenty degrees, the older woman shooting icy daggers with her eyes.

"Steady, darlin'. She can't hurt you," Dalton said as he gathered Amber's arm in his for support.

Amber was surprised by how much the woman's intense stare intimidated her. She had always felt as if Connie hated her, but today there was even more animosity to the hatred Connie projected. Amber felt an increase in her heart rate and fought to remain calm. Not for the first time, she found herself grateful for the calming effect Dalton had on her. Swallowing her fear, she met the woman's gaze head-on.

You have no power over me.

She continued the staring contest as Dalton guided her to the reception desk and waited for Racheal to slide open the glass that separated them.

"Miss Racheal, my wife and I had to step outside for a moment. Could you please let Mrs. Haddox know that we've returned?" Dalton said when the window finally opened. While he'd said it politely, there was a firmness in his tone, and he'd made sure to emphasize the word "wife."

Connie was out of her chair so quickly that it momentarily tipped backwards. She pushed past Dalton, pointing her shaky index finger at Amber. For the first time, Amber noticed the change. Normally a woman who took pride in her appearance, Connie looked as if she'd aged twenty years in the last four. Gray now replaced the brown in her hair, and the finger that was obnoxiously close to her face was in desperate need of a manicure. The lack of care showed in her clothes, which appeared to be standard off-the-rack clothing instead of the trendy designer apparel she normally wore. A surprise, since Amber had seen the woman work in her flower garden dressed much better than her current attire. It was obvious to Amber that Jeff's death had been hard on the woman. If it wasn't for the hate-filled eyes and finger dancing in front of her face, Amber might have felt compelled to ask if Connie was okay. The answer was no because when she spoke, her words were full of venom.

"How dare you come here and try to lay claim to my grandson. You are a selfish bitch, and you have no claim to Jeff's son."

Amber took a step back, and Dalton moved in between the two. When he spoke, his voice was surprisingly calm. "Ma'am, I can see you are upset, but that gives you no call to speak to my WIFE in that way. You will do good to remember that."

The meeting room door opened, and Walt stepped out, closing the door behind him. While Amber was shocked by the change in Connie, she couldn't get over the drastic change in her former father-in-law. The hair that was clinging to his scalp the last time she'd seen him was completely gone, replaced by a shiny, aged, spotted scalp. He'd always been small-framed, but he'd lost so much weight, his bones seemed to have trouble holding him straight. Her former in-laws looked as if they'd gone through a time machine, neither having fared well. Dalton was right. They were old.

Walt's presence went unacknowledged by Connie, who now turned her anger towards Dalton.

"Your wife. Your wife," she repeated with malice. "Your wife is nothing but a cheap, worthless slut. She claimed to have loved Jeff, yet the dirt didn't have a blade of grass growing on top when the two of you...you hillbillies got married. For all I know, the two of you had been seeing each other for years before his death."

Dalton removed his hat and ran a hand through his hair. He considered her for a moment before returning the black Stetson to his head. When he spoke, his voice was eerily calm. "Ma'am, the woman who raised me brought me up to be a gentleman. At no time in my life have I ever even considered raising my hand to a woman. Until now."

Amber reached for his arm. "She isn't worth it, Dalton."

"I know," he said with a sigh, "but all the same, I'd sure like to give her a good dunk in a rain barrel."

Walt snickered, hurriedly covering the sound with a cough. He stepped forward and gingerly took his wife by the arm. "Connie, I think we should go now."

"Aren't you going to come to my defense?" she asked, pulling away from him.

Walt looked at her as if she'd lost her mind. "Nope."

Connie whirled on her husband. "You are nothing but a weasel of a man. When did you lose your backbone?"

"The day I married you," he said with a shrug.

Connie's hand shot out and connected against Walt's cheek with such force that it sent him stumbling backwards. Dalton pushed past her, catching the man just before he hit the floor.

Realizing what she'd done, Connie was at his side, professing her apology. To her credit, she even managed a couple of tears. "Oh, Walt, I'm so sorry. I didn't mean to hit you."

This time, it was Walt who brushed her away. "There's no need for theatrics, dear. We both know this is not the first time you've hit me."

Walt leaned on Dalton's arm as he escorted him to a nearby chair and waited for him to sit.

Connie's eyes grew wide. "You know that is not true. I was just upset. I got caught up in the heat of the moment."

Amber turned towards the reception area. Racheal stood facing them, a phone to her ear. She could not hear the conversation, but the young girl was obviously upset, speaking low and waving her hands wildly as she spoke. Once again, she worried about the girl's age and lack of experience in a setting that could turn volatile.

She's not cut out for this job. Not yet, anyway.

Amber glanced at the door marked "meeting room." Surely Mrs. Haddox could hear the happenings.

And if she can, then so can Daxton.

The thought angered her as she pictured the boy hiding in a corner crying, frightened by the raised voices on the other side of the door.

Racheal lowered the phone, slipped from her sheltered cubicle, hurriedly disappearing behind the door marked "meeting room." Seconds later, the door reopened, and Judi Haddox emerged, looking none too pleased. The woman crossed the distance in six determined steps, her heels smacking angrily at the bottoms of her feet as she crossed the distance.

Dalton moved close to Amber, silently slipping his hand around hers.

"Could someone please tell me what the hell is going on out here?" Haddox said as she approached.

The request was met with blank stares.

Haddox stared pointedly at each person before rephrasing her question. "My receptionist has filled me in on the details. Not that she had to; the walls in this building are thin. Mr. Wilson, are you all right?"

"It's about time she showed up," Dalton whispered.

Amber nodded her agreement.

"Of course he is okay," Connie said heatedly.

"Mrs. Wilson, need I remind you there is a child behind those thin walls? You will keep your voice down. Mr. Wilson, I'll ask again, are you okay?" she said, directing her attention back to Walt.

Connie's lips pinched together as she waited for her husband to reply.

"Yes, I'm fine," Walt replied.

"I've already called the police. Do you need an ambulance?"

Amber looked up at Dalton. She was pretty sure her own expression mirrored the stunned look on his face.

The expression on Connie's face turned to one of complete horror. "Police?! We do not need the police. Look at him. He's fine."

"You assaulted him," Haddox said coolly.

"I got caught up in the heat of the moment and slapped him." Connie's voice belied the fear in her eyes.

Haddox stood firm. "No, Connie. You assaulted your husband, again."

Walt let out a deep sigh. "I can't do this anymore, Connie."

Connie looked at Amber, then back to her husband. "Shut up, Walter. This is not the place."

Walt leaned forward in his chair. "And when is the right time, Connie? After we get home? When there are no witnesses?"

"That's enough!" Connie said and took a step in his direction.

Dalton cut around her and stood between her and her husband.

Connie paused, appraising him. "You don't scare me."

Dalton remained silent.

"You think you are all high and mighty," Connie snarled. "We'll see if you still feel that way when we get custody of our grandchild."

Amber felt her stomach do a flip. If Connie hit Walt, what would keep her from hitting a child? *Jeff. Had his mother abused him? Was that why Heather had not offered Jeff's parents custody of their child?*

The outer door pushed open, and two uniformed officers stepped in. As Connie turned her attention to the new arrivals, all color drained from the woman's face.

Chapter Seventeen

The police escorted a tearful Connie from the building in handcuffs. Amber sat next to Dalton, leaning into him for support. Judi Haddox stood near where Walt was sitting. She'd approached both of them while the police were taking to Walt and Connie, assuring them that Daxton was all right and promised they would be allowed to see the child as soon as the mess was cleared up.

"She's been through so much lately," Walt said once Connie was out of earshot. "It wasn't always this bad. The occasional outburst. But since our son…"

"That's no excuse for hitting someone," Haddox said softly.

Walt sat rail straight and studied his hands. "I didn't believe Jeff. He told me that his mother hit him, but she never did it around me, so I didn't know how bad she could get. He was a child. Children get spankings."

He paused and looked at Amber. "Then when he married you, things changed. One day we were talking. I must have said something she didn't approve of, and bam, the woman hit me. I was so shocked, I couldn't move. I didn't say a word, just stood there staring in disbelief. I guess by not confronting her, I sort of gave her permission to continue. Because after that, she would hit me without provocation."

"Why didn't you tell Jeff?" Amber asked.

"I guess a part of me felt I deserved it. You know, kind of punishment for letting her hit him." Walt's eyes brimmed with tears.

Amber was torn as to whether she should go to him to offer comfort, but in the end, she remained in her chair. For the first time since marrying Jeff, she was grateful his parents had not taken an interest in Julie.

"I can't believe Jeff never told me about his mother."

"Maybe he didn't think you would believe him either," Walt said by way of explanation.

There was something in the way he said it. Maybe it was more the way he had looked at her, but a sudden dawning arose. She leaned closer to Dalton, swallowing the hurt. "But he told Heather, and that is why she was adamant that you and Connie not get custody of Daxton."

He nodded. "Connie was devastated at losing Jeff. Then neither Heather nor her parents would allow her to see the boy."

Haddox intervened. "But Michigan has grandparents' rights. She could have filed…"

Walt laughed. "Don't you think my wife didn't think of that? She called Heather up right after the boy was born. The girl was prepared. She'd already contacted an attorney. Told Connie that if she filed for visitation, she'd prove her unfit. Told her she'd make sure every one of her friends knew that she was an abuser. She even threw oil on the fire by telling Connie I could come see the boy, as long as I came alone."

"Did you?" the three of them asked at once.

"No good would have come of that," Walt said with a sigh. "Didn't matter, though. Connie stopped going to bingo, no more book club meetings. She just stayed at home. She stopped getting her hair colored. Not that I minded. But it was the other stuff. She stopped taking pride in the way she looked. She'd look in the mirror and then get angry, and when she got angry..."

"She would hit you," Haddox said.

Walt nodded, then turned towards Amber. "Then, a couple of days ago, we were watching the evening news, and there you were in handcuffs. You took up the whole screen, and she threw a glass at you. Missed, thankfully. It's the only TV we have."

Amber felt herself cringe but didn't offer comment.

"My wife didn't do anything wrong," Dalton said, taking her hand in his.

This time, Walt nodded in agreement. "That's what the news said. But they also went on to say that Amber had returned to town to get her son. That was the catalyst. It's no secret my wife disliked you. So when she heard you would be the one raising Jeff's son and she didn't even get to see him, well, she just came unhinged. Connie was livid, storming through the house and telling how she would have that child if it was the last thing she did. She didn't care if she had to destroy you to get him."

"Jesus, Walt. She hates me that much? All I did was marry her son."

"No, you took her son away from her," Walt corrected. "She loved her son."

"Loved him so much she beat him?"

Walt stood and gave a sheepish smile. "Sometimes people have a strange way of showing love."

"Where will you go now?" Amber asked.

"Home. After a trip to the police station to drop the charges."

"But what about..." Amber stopped when Haddox made eye contact, warning her off.

"Remember what we discussed, Mr. Wilson. You have the number to social services. Convince your wife to get into grief counseling, and if she lays a hand on you again, call the police. It is the only way this is ever going to end. And thank you for what you did here today. I know that it was difficult for you."

Walt patted his pocket and then turned his attention back to Amber, looking from her to Dalton as he spoke. "I am not proud of what I've done today. A man doesn't turn on his wife. It's just not done. But that boy in there didn't ask to be born, and he damn sure didn't ask to be jerked from home to home. The last thing he needs is to be dropped into a home where he will go through life afraid. I wasn't there for my son. I'm not going to make the same mistake with my grandson."

Walt approached them, reached a tentative hand to Dalton. "You seem to be doing a fine job of taking care of my son's wife. I'll trust you'll do the same for his son."

Dalton stood and grasped Walt's hand. "I will raise him as my own son, sir, no worries about that."

Walt nodded, looked at Amber as if he had more to say, but finally left without another word.

"I am not sure what surprises me most, that Connie is an abuser or that Walt is dropping the charges," Amber said as soon as Walt breached the door.

Haddox sat, slipped off her heels, and rubbed the bottoms of her feet. "I hope you don't mind. My feet are killing me. When I get home, I'm throwing these in the trash."

When no one objected, she continued.

"Your father-in-law and I had a nice chat before he came out. He told me about his wife and agreed to press charges."

"Ex father-in-law," Amber clarified. "How did he know she was going to slap him?"

"He didn't. I placed the call while he was still in the room with me. It wasn't until my... until Racheal called me that I knew she had slapped him. To be honest, it was icing on the cake."

Haddox pointed towards multiple cameras.

"We have the assault on tape. That, along with Mr. Wilson's testimony, if it even gets to that point, will ensure that you and your husband have no obstacles adopting Daxton."

Amber felt her heart flutter. "You mean we get to take him home?"

Haddox appraised them both briefly. "As long as today's meeting goes well, yes."

Amber felt hopeful for the first time in days. "Today?"

A frown fleeted across the woman's face. "Let's see how the meeting goes, okay?"

This time, it was Dalton who spoke. "And if the meeting doesn't go well?"

Haddox returned the heels to her feet and stood with a groan. "I hate these shoes. I hate this office. Hell, I even hate this job. I'm done. When I leave, I'm taking all my belongings. My replacement will return on Monday. If that child is still here when you leave, he will be placed back in foster care. Not with the same family, but the process will continue. If he is with you, in another state, then your attorney will be able to put up enough roadblocks that they will not be able to remove him. You have permission from the mom. The maternal grandparents are on your side, and unless someone else climbs out from under a rock, the law is on your side. Now, unless you have any more questions, how about we go meet your son? My feet are killing me, and I'd like to sit down."

Chapter Eighteen

Amber followed Dalton and Haddox into the room, eager to get the first glimpse of her son. Her stomach did a flop. She couldn't remember a time when she'd been this excited. Daxton was sitting in the corner, his back to them. He was small, wore jeans, a blue sweatshirt, and sneakers on feet that couldn't reach the floor. He had a mop of sandy blonde hair and a pair of headphones that looked three sizes too large for his head. Whatever he was listening to, he seemed to enjoy, as his little legs dangled to the beat of a sound only he could hear. The second she saw him, her hands trembled. She felt waves of nausea, excitement, and pure unconditional love. It was like giving birth without the pain. She longed to run to him, scoop him into her aching arms, and smother him with kisses. One glance at her husband and she knew his feelings mirrored her own. She felt Dalton's hand squeeze hers. She smiled, blinking back tears.

As the trio approached the boy, Racheal reached over and removed his headphones.

"Daxton, this is your..." The girl looked to Haddox, who closed her eyes briefly, then nodded her approval. "This is your mommy and daddy," she said with conviction.

Daxton turned, and for the first time, she could see his face. It was slimmer than it appeared in the photo, his complexion milky white and flawless, right down to his little button nose. He stared up at them, his green eyes framed with long lashes, and at that moment, Amber realized he looked exactly like Julie when she was his age. He blinked, sized them up, reached for the headphones, and declared, "No mommy! No daddy!"

His words were a direct hit to her heart. She fought back tears as he replaced the headphones and refused to look at either of them.

"Well, that went well," Haddox said, walking to a nearby chair. She sat, removed her shoes, and waved a palm towards the other chair, which Amber reluctantly accepted.

Dalton turned towards the door.

"I never had you pegged for a quitter," Haddox said to a retreating Dalton.

"I left something in the truck," he replied before leaving the room.

The second he left, Amber knew where he was headed.

The horses and the mystery bag, whatever is in it. I hope it works.

"So, how did the two of you meet, if you don't mind me asking?" Haddox said, drawing Amber's attention.

Amber felt her face flush.

"I was at the fairgrounds, and this cowboy stopped and asked me a question." She'd been hiding from a guy she'd shared a brief encounter with. It was no more than a quick make-out session, the by-product of too much wine, but the guy had taken it as more. So there she was hiding in the car when Dalton pulled into the lot. He got out wearing tight-fitting jeans and a snug t-shirt that showcased his lean, muscular arms. He was wearing boots and sported a day-old beard under a low-slung black cowboy hat. For Amber, it was lust at first sight. She felt her face flush at the memory.

"Must have been some question," Haddox said with a snicker.

"He asked me where the groundskeeper was. Everything sounds better when said with a smooth southern drawl," Amber added when Haddox lifted her eyes.

This time, it was the social worker's turn to blush. "Yes, I've noticed."

Both women giggled as Dalton returned to the room. With the exception of the facial hair, Dalton looked the same as the first time she'd laid eyes on him.

He held the bag up for her to see. "Want to play with me?"

"Oh my," Haddox said in reply.

"Exactly," Amber said and followed Dalton to a spot near Daxton. He sat on the floor, holding out a hand to Amber. *What is he up to?* she thought, taking his hand and lowering to his level. Dalton made a big show of opening one of the two bags he'd retrieved and pulled out the horses one at a time. Amber looked past him to see that Daxton was watching them with great interest. Dalton took each horse and went to great lengths to make playing with stationary plastic horses look like the most fun he'd ever had.

"Come on, darlin', don't let me have all the fun," he said, handing her a horse.

"You are a nut job," she said, taking the horse.

He took one of the horses and chased another around the floor. "Is it working?"

Amber peeked at Daxton through hair that had fallen over her face. The child had his hands on his headphones, straining to see what they were doing.

Amber smiled at Dalton. "Actually, I think it is."

Dalton took the black horse that looked like his, gave it a voice, and chased Amber's horse around her leg.

"You are really having fun, aren't you?" Amber giggled.

"I like horses," he said, causing her to blush once more.

The child removed the headphones and ran to where they were sitting on the floor. He scrambled to the spot between them, scooped up the remaining horses, and raced them over Dalton's leg. "Daxton do it!"

Dalton made some horse noises that Daxton quickly attempted to mimic. Dalton laughed and picked up the black horse. "That's Daddy's horse."

"Daddy's horse," Daxton repeated.

Dalton took the painted horse from Amber, pointed at her, and said, "This is Mama's horse."

Daxton took the horse from Dalton. "Mama's horse."

Dalton picked up the other black horse.

"Daddy's horse," Daxton said, pointing to Dalton.

"No, this is Julie's horse. See? It has white on its nose and legs," Dalton said, pointing out the difference.

"Julie's horse," Daxton said, tossing it aside and reaching for the smaller palomino. "Horse?"

"You are a smart one," Dalton said, beaming. "This is Katie's horse."

"Katie's horse." Once again, he tossed the horse and reached for the last one, holding it up and blinking his puzzlement. "Horse?"

Dalton held out his hands, and Amber's heart melted as Daxton climbed into Dalton's lap. He looked down at the horse and repeated his question. "Horse?"

"That is Daxton's horse," Dalton said with a smile.

Daxton's eyes grew wide as he stared at the small plastic horse.

"Daxton's horse," he said, clinging tightly to the spotted horse.

Dalton chanced a hug, his hat creating a shadow on the floor as he hugged the boy close.

Daxton craned his head backwards. "Hat?"

"Daddy's hat," Dalton replied.

"No. Daxton's hat," Daxton said, reaching for the hat.

"No, Daddy's hat," Dalton replied, pulling back.

Amber bit her lip to suppress a giggle. She knew how much Dalton treasured his hat, but the man was in danger of a major setback. Not only was Daxton three, but it also appeared he was used to getting his way.

As if reading her mind, Daxton lowered his hands and crossed his arms, a pout forming on his lips. Just as it looked as if they'd lost their edge, Dalton reached for the second bag. Daxton relaxed his arms, his anger replaced with curiosity. A curiosity she shared.

Dalton opened the bag and made quite the show of fishing for the contents. Daxton waited, his face anxious to see what treasures Dalton would produce.

Amber was just about ready to say something when a voice called out from behind.

"Oh, for the love of God, just show us what's in the bag," Haddox said, echoing her thoughts.

Dalton sighed and finally withdrew his arm from the bag. When his hand appeared, it was holding a small replica of the hat he was wearing on his head. Dalton's smile reached his eyes as he placed the hat on top of the boy's head. "Daxton's hat!"

Daxton removed the hat, gave it a once over, and returned it to his head. He reached for the grey horse, pretending it was running along Dalton's leg. As he reached the bottom of Dalton's pants, his face took on a quizzical expression. He pulled up the end of Dalton's jeans and exposed the boots he was wearing. Releasing the hem, he grabbed his own jeans and stuck out his foot. "Daxton's boots?"

Dalton removed his hat and ran a hand through his hair. When he looked to Amber for help, she answered with a shrug. Obviously, Dalton had underestimated this child.

"We will get you some boots, son," he said and returned the hat to his head.

Chapter Nineteen

Amber watched as Katie and Daxton played in the playroom, the boy running from toy to toy, Katie chasing after him like a little mother hen. They must have been at it for some time as toys were everywhere. Clancy lay in the corner, panting, his eyes following them around the sunny room. Clancy saw her and wagged his tail, but made no move to rise. All those years of chasing him and apparently all the dog needed was a family to help calm him down, Amber observed as the two children played together. It had only been two days since they'd arrived back at Sunset Meadows with Daxton, and already he fit in as if he'd lived there from birth. So far, the only point of discontent was that Daxton still felt he needed a pair of boots, even going so far as finding Dalton's discarded boots the evening prior and trying them on for size. Slipping his tiny feet inside, he raced into the room, declaring them his boots. The sight of the child trying to fill Dalton's boots made everyone laugh. Amber smiled just thinking about it.

Katie's face lit up when she saw her. "Hi, Momma."

"Hi, Momma," Daxton repeated, making Amber's heart swell even more.

"Hello to you both," she said, entering the room. "Where is your sister?"

"She is outside in the east barn with Jake. They were whispering, and she told me I had to go back inside and play with Daxton."

"Whispering, huh?" *I hope that is all they are doing in the barn.* "What were they whispering about?"

Katie's eyes grew wide. "I didn't hear."

Sure you didn't. "Well, I think I'll go have a talk with her. Are you and Daxton okay playing in here?"

"Yes, Momma," Katie replied.

"Yes, Momma," Daxton mimicked.

"Okay, if you need anything, Miss Maggie is right down the hall, and Miss Barbara is in the kitchen."

"Okay, Momma."

"Okay, Momma," Daxton repeated.

Amber beamed as she left the room. She wasn't sure how long the honeymoon stage would last, but for now, she was happy to see the two kids getting along. She started down the hallway towards the front door when Katie's voice called to her.

"Momma, what is a receiving blanket?"

"It's a baby blanket. Why do you ask?"

The little girl's face scrunched in confusion. "Because that is what Julie was whispering about. She told Jake she needed to get some receiving blankets."

That's odd. "Maybe you misunderstood. If Julie and Jake were in the horse barn, maybe they were talking about a horse blanket."

"Oh," Katie said and disappeared back inside the playroom.

Or, she could have said "receiving blanket." But why?

Amber stepped out onto the front porch, stood for a moment drinking in the morning sun and closing her eyes to let its warmth embrace her. The days were getting warmer, but the mornings still had a welcomed coolness to the air. *There is a nap in my future.*

"Hello, beautiful," Dalton's voice called from across the way. "Feeling better?"

Amber opened her eyes, turned in the direction of his voice, and saw the concern on his face. "Much better. Don't tell Miss Barbara, but I think her goulash got the better of me."

"Do we need to hire a chef?" he asked, closing the distance.

"No, I don't think it was the stew as much as all the stress from dealing with Jeff's parents and traveling lately. I'm pretty sure if there were anything wrong with the stew, I would not be the only one feeling ill."

"You have a point there," he said, wrapping his arms around her and kissing her fully on the lips.

"Mmm, see? I'm better already." She always felt energized when in his embrace.

"How's Daxton?" Dalton asked, looking towards the house.

"He is great. He and Katie are in the playroom."

"I think I'll take them riding later. Want to come?"

"You're not going to put him on a horse by himself, are you?" Amber regretted her words the minute she said them. For years, Dalton and his only sister, Lana, were on the outs, stemming from a misunderstanding about how to raise his daughter, Katie. In the end, both Lana and Dalton were only trying to ensure the child's safety, something that was never truly in question when it came to Dalton.

He laughed. "You sound like my sister."

Amber bit her lip. "Sorry, it is the mom in me."

"You know I would never risk my child... any child," he corrected.

"He's as much your child as he is mine, and I know you wouldn't."

"So, about that ride?"

"I'd love to. I have something to check on first," she said, gazing towards the barn.

Dalton turned to see where she was looking. "Problem?"

Maybe. "Probably not, it's just that Katie told me she heard Julie and Jake whispering by the horse barn. Something about blankets," she said, leaving out the fact that they were talking about baby blankets.

"Remind me to have a chat with Katie about tattling."

Amber laughed. "I think we should hold off on that for a while."

"Oh?"

"They are teenagers. It might not be bad to have a little spy."

"OH," he said with understanding. "Either way, I don't think they are out there now. I asked Jake to get some supplies."

"Was Julie with him when you spoke to him?"

"I didn't see her. To be honest, she could have been. Jake was just stepping out of the barn when I caught up with him, said he'd been checking on the new foal."

The foal. Of course. They were probably looking for soft blankets for the new little filly.

"Something I said?"

"You called me beautiful," she said, stepping around the truth.

"Because you are," he said, kissing her with more feeling.

She leaned into him, wishing they had time for more but knowing now was not the time. Reluctantly, she pulled away.

"I love you. But if you don't stop kissing me like that, neither one of us is going to get anything done today."

Dalton ran a finger around the neckline of her top. "Maybe we should take the day off."

Amber felt torn. "Your offer is tempting, sir, but I have some things I really need to get done today if I'm going to go shopping with Robin tomorrow."

"Foiled by a shopping trip."

She giggled. "Well, if you'd prefer to take Daxton shopping for new clothes and boots…"

Dalton removed his hat and ran a hand through his silky hair. "That boy is not going to stop until he gets those boots."

"He wants to be just like his dad," Amber said and was rewarded with a huge smile from Dalton.

"Then, by all means, go about your day." He turned her around and swatted her on the bottom to send her on her way.

Amber headed to the east barn to look for Julie. She was met with several nickers from outstretched heads as she entered, but still no sign of Julie. She heard a noise in one of the stalls on the far side of the barn and walked in that direction. When she approached, she was relieved to see Carl, the ranch foreman, bottle-feeding one of the new fillies. There had been six born in the months since the first early spring birth.

"Morning, Mrs. Amber, something I can do for you?" he said when she approached.

"No, looks like you've got your hands full."

"This little fellow is not gaining weight. The mare doesn't seem to have enough milk, so we are supplementing. Want to give it a go?"

Amber raised her eyes at him. "Do you mean would I like to feed the baby while you go take one of your cigarette breaks? Not going to happen. You know I promised Thelma Jo I'd do my best to get you to quit."

His face turned sullen. "Why is it women are so intent to change a man? Why can't she just love me for my rugged good looks and charm?"

Amber let her gaze drift across Carl's ragged jeans, wrinkled flannel shirt, which looked as if he'd spent a week in it, and soiled boots. His face was in dire need of a shave, limp hair extended below his worn hat, and his face showed he was more in need of a nap than she. "Do me a favor, Carl."

"What's that?" he asked, switching the bottle to his other hand.

"Ask me that question again when I know you haven't been sleeping in your clothes."

Carl lifted his arm and sniffed. "Been up with the lad here most of the night."

"Do you want me to finish feeding him while you take a break?" Her offer was genuine.

He thought about it, then shook his head. "Naw, you're right. I'd just use the break to light another cigarette. Wouldn't want you to have my early demise weighing on your conscience."

"Well, if you change your mind, let me know," she said, looking around the barn. "You haven't seen Julie, have you?"

He shook his head once more. "Not much of a view from in here."

Amber left the barns and decided to head back to the house. She peeked in on Katie and Daxton before heading up the stairs in search of Julie. The teen's door was closed. She knocked then pushed it open to display an empty room. The sound of water running let Amber know Julie was in the shower. She sat on the bed, decided it was too enticing, and moved to the reading chair in the corner. I'm a regular Goldilocks," Amber laughed, lowering herself into the cozy chair.

She closed her eyes and felt herself relax. Opening them, she shifted to a less comfortable position, glanced at the side table, and picked up the book from the table. As she lifted it, she noticed the pages were separated, giving the book a bowed appearance. *What on earth is she using as a bookmark?* Opening the book, her breath caught at the sight of the little pregnancy wand. Her hands trembled as she turned it over, exposing two pink lines. One bold, the other barely visible, but its message extremely clear.

Her baby girl was pregnant.

Chapter Twenty

Amber's first instinct was to storm into Julie's bathroom and demand answers. Instead, she leaned into the cozy chair for support. All thoughts of a nap forgotten, her mind now raced, seeking answers. *How far along? Not too far, as there are no visible signs of the pregnancy. Still, it is late spring, and bulky clothes can hide a lot. Who is the father? Jake is the most logical choice. We should fire the fricker. No, he is responsible for this mess; he will have to remain here to help. Providing Dalton doesn't kill the boy first. Boy, the kid is almost twenty. That makes him an adult. Statutory rape?* Amber decided to file that one away until later. Where had they done the deed? She cast a glance to the bed. Would they be so bold to have had sex in Julie's room? Probably not; it would have been a great risk to sneak into the room with so many people living in the house. The barns? Her mind drifted to the conversation with Carl. "Not much of a view from in here." Meaning not much chance of being seen as long as the two were being discreet. That thought conjured up visuals that she quickly extinguished from her mind. It was bad enough that they had done the deed, she was not going to imagine the way they went about doing it. Still, she had questions. Was he gentle with her the first time? First time? Did that mean there was more than one? Most likely. Rarely did someone get pregnant during their first encounter. Her mind retreated to a younger self standing in the bathroom, holding a wand. She was seventeen at the time. *The same age as Julie.* It had been tough, but at least Jeff had done the honorable thing. She laughed; it was probably the only honorable thing he'd ever done when it came to her. But even with Jeff's financial support, it had been difficult. She was young and had no clue how to raise a child. Thankfully, Julie had a network of people who would help with the child. *Would Jake insist they get married? Can I really allow her to go down the same path that I did? Do I even have a say in what she does anymore? She's nearly eighteen. If I push her away now, she may take the baby and never come back.*

Amber bit her lip, anger bubbling below the surface. It was she who should be pregnant, not her seventeen-year-old daughter. She was just a baby herself. Julie should be dating, going to the prom, heading off to college in a few years.

She should be doing all the things I never got to do.

She should be babysitting, not raising a child of her own. She looked at the book in her lap, a YA showing two teenagers on the cover, an innocent story of a teen romance. *Innocent, my ass.* She threw the book across the room, hitting the bathroom door, which quickly opened. Julie emerged wrapped in a towel, another covering her head. Holding the lower towel in place, the teen bent, gathered up the book, a questioning look crossing her face.

"What the heck, Mom. I thought you taught us to respect books."

"I taught you to respect your body too," Amber replied heatedly.

Julie took a step backwards. "What the heck is that supposed to mean?"

"Cut the bullshit, Julie. I know your little secret."

"My secret?"

"I said cut with the bullshit," Amber said, holding up the wand. She was going about it the wrong way, but she just couldn't help herself. "I thought I taught you better than this. I thought you would have learned from my mistakes."

Amber regretted her words the instant they came out of her mouth.

"So now I'm a mistake?" The hurt in Julie's voice was unmistakable.

"That is not what I meant, and you know it," Amber said softly.

"It's what you said."

"No, I said not using protection was a mistake. Getting pregnant at an early age was a mistake. Having you was the best thing that ever happened to me." Too late, Amber could already see the wall that had gone up between them. Striving to remain calm, she switched tactics.

"Who's the father?"

Julie blinked her surprise. "You have to ask?"

Another grave mistake. "I'm sorry. I figure it was Jake, but apparently, there is a lot I don't know."

Like the fact that my seventeen-year-old is having sex.

"Jake is the only boy I've even kissed," Julie said, blinking back tears.

Amber held up the wand. "From the looks of this, I'd say you've done more than kiss."

Julie hesitated, opened her mouth to reply, and shook her head. Whatever she was about to say was lost. Instead, she removed the towel from her head and ran her fingers through wet hair to remove the tangles. Amber watched her, so young, so innocent, so not ready to become a mom. Amber tried to judge how far along Julie was, not far enough to display a bulge in the tightly wound towel.

"Does Jake know?" Amber asked softly.

Julie peered at her. "I told him this morning. I asked him not to say anything to anyone."

"What did he say?"

Another moment of hesitation as Julie considered her words. "He said he figured it would happen sooner or later."

"Sooner or later? How long have the two of you been intimate?"

Julie shrugged.

"So, what are the two of you planning to do?"

"Do?"

God, the girl was trying her nerves. "Yes, do. What are you going to do about the baby?"

Julie's lips curved into a smile. "I guess we thought you would raise it."

Amber felt as if she'd been slapped. First, the blatant disregard for everything Amber had gone through as a teenage mother, and now, to casually suggest that Amber and Dalton raise the child. Sure they would help. Be there to give moral and financial support, but Julie was acting as if she held no responsibility in the matter. How had she failed this bad at parenting?

Where did I go wrong?

Julie tossed the towel on the bed and walked to her closet. Stepping inside, she closed the door. When she emerged a few moments later, she was wearing jeans and a loose-fitting sweater. For all appearances, she was a normal seventeen-year-old child.

No, not a child. Not anymore.

Amber rubbed her temples, trying to relieve a headache that was beginning to take hold.

"I'm going to go for a walk."

"Where to?"

"I'm going to talk to Jake."

"Talk?"

"Holy crap, Mom, do you think I'm running out to have sex?"

"I don't know what you are going to do. I thought I knew you. But after this, I just don't know anymore."

"That's because you think everything that goes wrong in this world is a reflection on you. You come in here nosing around in my room and for what? What were you looking for?"

Amber was shocked at Julie's sudden defensiveness. "I came in here looking for you."

"You heard me in the shower. Why didn't you just come back?"

"I was tired. I sat down and then I saw the pregnancy test and I wanted to ask you about it."

"No, you wanted to yell at me about it. You didn't ask anything. You started yelling at me the second I came out of the bathroom. One minute I'm in the shower, the next I'm getting the third degree."

"How dare you make me out to be the bad guy here? I'm your mother. I care about you. You're supposed to come to me when you have a problem. We used to be so close. What happened to us?"

Tears trickled down Julie's cheek. "You got married. You have another family now. You used to talk to me, but now you keep everything to yourself. You didn't even tell me about Daxton."

Amber rubbed her temples again. "Julie, I was wrong keeping that from you. From everyone, but I thought we'd gotten past that."

"We talked, but obviously there are still plenty more secrets," Julie said with a nod to the little plastic wand.

"We are not finished here," Amber said when Julie started for the door. "We need to figure this out. We need to let the family know."

"Then call a family meeting. Let me know when and I'll be there," Julie said and left the room without bothering to close the door.

Chapter Twenty-One

They rode down the narrow, tree-lined path, single file, Dalton leading the way, Katie Mae following, and Amber bringing up the rear on her horse, Wish. Clancy ran ahead, weaving on and off the path, sniffing everything in sight. Daxton rode in front of Dalton, chattering away about horses, birds, trees, and various other things that caught his eye.

Most of Sunset Meadows had been cleared to make way for pastures, large plots of lush grass divided into sections with acres of fencing surrounding the whole estate. There were plenty of large shade trees near the house, and along the long paved driveway that led from the road to the main house. Dalton had also purposely left trees in multiple locations around the horse ranch to allow for peaceful trail rides shielded against the heat of the day. Today was not one of those heat-filled days. In fact, today, Amber preferred the heat of the sun to the chill of the darkened path.

"Everyone okay back there?" Dalton asked over his shoulder.

"I'm good, Daddy," Katie answered, giving her horse a tap with her legs to encourage her to catch up.

While Amber didn't hear it, she was pretty sure Daxton echoed his father's words. Amber was pleased with the active role Dalton had taken with Daxton. As she'd seen him do with Julie, Dalton talked to him as an adult, patiently telling him everything he was doing and why. Daxton looked up to Dalton, soaking up every word.

She had yet to tell Dalton about Julie, wanting to get him as far away from Jake as possible before breaking the news. Jake was like a son to Dalton; hell, to her too, for that matter. But now, the boy had betrayed both of their trust in a way she wasn't sure could be mended. Amber was so deep in thought that she didn't notice they'd cleared the woods until Dalton spoke to her.

"You are a million miles away," Dalton said, reining his horse closer.

She knew she'd have to tell him sooner or later. It looked like it was going to be even sooner than she'd hoped. She let out a sigh and felt tears spring to her eyes.

"Julie's pregnant," she blurted.

Dalton pulled his horse to an abrupt stop.

Daxton kicked his little feet, urging the horse to move. "Giddy up, horsey!"

Dalton ignored the child's demands, much to Daxton's dismay. "How?"

Amber raised her eyebrows.

"Okay, when?"

"I'm not sure. I just found out a couple of hours ago."

"A couple of hours. Why didn't you tell me?"

"I was waiting for the right time." *And I was scared that you might strangle Jake.*

Daxton leaned back into Dalton's chest and kicked the horse's neck once more. "Horsey won't go, Daddy!"

"Just a minute, son," Dalton said firmly enough that Daxton stilled.

Amber had to give the man credit; he was staying a lot calmer than she had. Then again, that was one of the things she loved about him.

"Jake?" Dalton asked.

"So it seems."

"You didn't ask?"

"Oh, I asked... Oh, Dalton, I went about the whole thing the wrong way. Why is it I keep making a mess of things?" Amber said tearfully.

"Mommy, you sad?" Daxton asked, looking at her.

Amber wiped at the tears. "Yes, baby. Mommy's a little sad."

"Kisses?" Daxton asked, leaning sideways.

"You blow Mommy a kiss, and I'll catch it," Amber said. "Here, watch." She placed a hand on her lips, kissed her palm, then, turning her hand upside down, blew the kiss in his direction.

Dalton raised a hand to catch the invisible kiss. A mistake, as Daxton started crying. "Daddy no kisses," Daxton wailed.

Dalton placed his hand on the boy's cheek. "There, now you have Mommy's kiss."

To Amber's surprise, it worked, and Daxton stopped crying. "Horsey go?"

"Horsey go," Dalton said, turning his horse in the direction of where Katie Mae, who'd gone ahead, was waiting in the clearing. Reaching her, Dalton dismounted, reached for Daxton, and walked over to Katie Mae.

"Do me a favor, Little Bit. Lead Daxton around in a circle to let him get the feel of being in the saddle by himself."

Katie slid off her horse and held the reins of her large palomino, obviously excited to have been taxed with such an important job. "Sure, Daddy."

"Keep close and hold tight to the reins.

And, you," he said, placing Daxton on the saddle. "You hold on to the saddle horn and don't let go."

Daxton gripped the knob on the front of the saddle and kicked his legs, delighted to be on the big horse by himself. "Go, horsey," he shouted as Katie started walking.

Amber smiled for the first time in hours. Any other horse she would have objected, but that beige mare had a heart of gold and the gentleness of a lamb.

She dismounted, tossing the reins over her mare. Keeping an eye on the two children, she spoke. "You are taking this well."

"Honestly, I'm just trying to figure out how I'm going to castrate Jake without going to jail," Dalton said, keeping his voice low.

"I'm pretty sure we are past that point," Amber replied.

"It explains one thing, though," Dalton said, looking at her.

"Which is?"

"Before we left, Jake told me he needed to go home for the day. When I asked him why, he told me it was personal. I can't remember the last time he asked for a day off, especially one without a reason."

"I'm pretty sure after my blow up with Julie, she warned him that I was going to tell you. He'd probably prefer to miss the day's pay than face you."

"He'll do more than face me."

"You know you can't kill him, don't you?" While she would have liked to strangle him, killing him seemed a bit extreme.

"I know. But how are we going to deal with this? Abortion is not an option. Neither is adoption. Not with our grandchild."

His words washed over them. They were going to be grandparents! Amber felt the color leave her face. A wave of nausea rushed over her. Her mouth watered as she fought to control the bile. Unable to control it any longer, she bent over and threw up, just missing Dalton's boots. Dalton reached for her, and she stopped him.

"I'm okay. I was feeling better until all this crap with Julie. Just my luck, Julie's pregnant and I'm the one with morning sickness. That or I'm getting an ulcer."

He gave her a look that said "I really wish I could help, but I have no clue what I'm supposed to do." "I'm pretty sure I'm right there with you."

She moved away from the smell, sat on the ground, and motioned for him to join her. Once he'd done so, she told him about how she'd come to find the wand, her confrontation with Julie, and how Julie had told her to call a family meeting.

"So the question is, do we listen to our irresponsible daughter, or do we wait until everyone starts asking questions?" Amber said.

Dalton chewed on that for a moment. "If she wants to tell the world, it has to be her decision. Like it or not, she is an adult now."

"She's seventeen."

"Even so, she's going to find out she has to start making adult decisions. First and foremost, she needs to take responsibility for her actions. That means she will be the one to tell the family she is pregnant."

Amber nodded, and Dalton took hold of her hand. "But... our job, as parents, is to protect our little girl. We are in this together, Amber Mae, we will be there when she tells everyone, and we will be there when she asks for our help in raising this child. It's what families.do."

"How did I ever get so lucky?" She'd asked him that question a million times, and he always responded with the same simple answer.

"You were born," he said, kissing the back of her hand.

Chapter Twenty-Two

"So tell me again why the kid doesn't have any clothes," Robin said as Amber handed her another outfit to hold.

Amber sifted through the rack, pulled out a pair of jeans, reconsidered, and added three more to the growing pile. "I'm sure he has more than what was in the backpack he came with, but to be honest, I don't care. The last thing I'm going to do is rattle the cage looking for clothes when we can afford to buy him what he needs. We are biding our time until we can legally adopt Daxton."

"Any idea when that will be?"

"Mr. Grether has filed the paperwork, so things are moving forward." She held up another outfit, seeing Robin's disapproving expression she returned the set to the rack. "It's so much easier to buy for little girls."

Robin shifted the pile of clothes she held. "You have enough here to fill a dresser. How much more does the kid need? Besides, it's getting warmer. How practical are jeans?"

Amber studied the clothes she'd gathered. Robin was right. Daxton would outgrow most of what she'd picked before he even had a chance to wear them. She returned two of the jeans and most of the other items Robin held to the rack, keeping a few of the dressier outfits for special occasions. She looked at the new pile and sighed. They'd been shopping for two hours and now only had a handful of things. Thankfully, Dalton had convinced her to leave Daxton with him and Maggie. The child would have been bored out of his mind by now. She moved to the summer clothes, found a display of t-shirts, and proceeded to select a size five in every design. Satisfied, she moved to the opposite side and gathered up shorts to match.

"That's it. I'm going to find a cart," Robin said when Amber handed them over to her.

Amber thumbed through the clothes, pulled out a couple of dressier short sets, and looked around for Robin, who was nowhere in sight. She continued moving through the department, gathering up pajamas, socks, and underwear. Daxton was in the end stages of potty-training, although he still had the occasional accident. She thumbed through the underwear, decided on six packages, and went in search of Robin.

Passing the baby section, Amber drifted down the first aisle. She stared at the mixes of pastels before settling on several ambiguous sleepers. As she had done in the toddler section, she began moving down the aisle, gathering things along the way. Seeing a yellow receiving blanket, she reached for it and suddenly everything she was holding dislodged from her grip, landing in a pile on the floor at her feet. Ignoring the mess, she plucked the blanket from the shelf and stood there running her fingers through the soft fabric. She was still standing there when Robin found her.

"Okay, spill it, girlfriend," Robin said, pulling her out of her trance.

"Just having a mental breakdown, that's all," Amber said, swiping tears that were now trickling down her face.

Robin pushed the cart to the side and lowered to the floor. She motioned for Amber to join her. Amber did and began picking up the items she'd dropped, carefully folding each one.

"Having second thoughts about adopting the kid?"

"Daxton? No, he is adorable," Amber said, folding a shirt.

Robin picked up a newborn sleeper, holding it up for Amber to see. "A bit small for an almost four-year-old, don't you think?"

Amber took it from her. "It's not for him."

Robin glanced at Amber's midsection and smiled. "I've been waiting for you to tell me."

"I'm not pregnant." Amber's words gave way to a fresh set of tears.

"Well, that is a surprise. You barely ate anything for breakfast. You look pale, and you are emotional as shit."

"All symptoms of stress," Amber said sullenly.

"Okay, you love the new kid. You are shopping for newborn clothes, but you are not pregnant. So who is all this baby stuff for?"

Before Amber could answer, a woman appeared in the aisle. She had a swell to her belly and a disgusted look on her face.

"Surely the two of you could find a more acceptable place to gab," she said and lifted her leg as if she was going to step over them.

Robin glared up at the woman. "If you don't want to end up on the floor with us, I'd suggest you go around."

The woman retracted her leg and backed from the aisle without another word.

Amber looked over her shoulder. "What if she needed something from this aisle?"

"Her stomach wasn't that big. She has time," Robin said with a shrug. "Now tell me what is going on."

"Julie's pregnant."

Robin's eyes grew wide. "Oh shit!"

"Oh shit is right."

"Who's the dad? When did it happen? What did Dalton say?"

Amber picked up another outfit, carefully folding it. "Jake."

"The hot little redhead?"

Amber stared at her.

"Well, he is a cutie. If you like red hair, which, I obviously do since I married a redhead. So how far along is she?"

"I'm not sure. Not too far. She isn't showing yet. Not that I can see anyway. We didn't talk much. I kind of lost it, yelled at her, and she shut down. She told me to call a family meeting, and she would share the news then."

"Did you?"

"It's scheduled for tonight. Want to come?"

"I wouldn't miss it for the world. Will the rest of the family mind if I am there?"

"You are family too."

Robin picked up a blanket and handed it to her to fold and grabbed another for herself. "You are mad, aren't you?"

"That Julie's pregnant? Damn right I'm mad. I've been where she is. She's nearly the same age as I was when I got pregnant with her."

"I know you are mad about that, but I meant about the fact that it is her and not you?"

Amber let out a long breath. "It should have been me."

"I know, girlfriend. But you need to channel that anger. Julie needs your support now. Does she know you and Dalton have been trying to have a kid?"

Amber thought for a minute. "Probably not. We didn't announce it."

"Good. The last thing you need is for Julie to feel guilty that she is having a baby and you're not. "

"I know. Can you believe she actually told me that she figured me and Dalton would raise this child?"

"Would you consider it? Raising the baby?"

"To tell you the truth, it pissed me off when she said it, and I'm not sure why."

"Simple. You were looking at yourself. You didn't get the easy button. You took the only path you had, and it sucked. Can you imagine how different your life would be if you'd had other options?"

"You mean if Mom were still alive and offered to help me with the baby instead? I have thought about it. Maybe I wouldn't have met Jeff, but if I had, I'm not sure anything would have turned out different. I was young and, at the time, I thought I loved Jeff. Hell, I thought he loved me too, but you see how that turned out."

Robin scooped up the rest of the items on the floor and tossed them into the basket. "I don't know why we are bothering to fold this stuff. It all needs to be put in the wash anyway."

Taking her friend's lead, Amber tossed the items she was holding in the cart. She placed her hands on the handle. "You know, I hate this. Hate that Julie is pregnant, but she needs to be held responsible for her actions."

"Like marrying Jake?"

"No... God, I hope not. Don't get me wrong, I like Jake. Well, I used to...I hope they don't see marriage as the only option."

"Okay, so I know how you feel about abortion, but surely you are not going to suggest adoption."

"Of course not. I just don't want them to think that getting married is the only way to go. We can all pitch in to help, and with Jake still working at the ranch, he can chip in and do his part as well."

"I'm surprised the boy still has a job. So, if things continue as they are, how can you make sure this is not going to happen again? You know how kids are; they sneak around at first, but then when the secret is out, they don't feel the need to hide their relationship anymore. First, they steal a kiss in front of you, and the next thing you know, you'll be cleaning the bathroom and find red pubic hairs on the soap."

"Ewwww." The thought made Amber's stomach churn.

Robin laughed. "The boy is going to end up moving in. You mark my words, and if he's sharing a bed, you will end up with a half a dozen red-headed babies running around the house."

And just like that, Amber could picture it, little-redheaded babies everywhere. Running through the house calling her by name. Granny, come here. Granny, I need you. Then Daxton was in the mix, running with them laughing and calling her Granny. He would too, just like Katie Mae did when she heard the others calling her Mom.

Damnit, I'm too young to be a granny!

She shook her head to rid herself of the vision. "That's not going to happen."

"And just how do you think you will stop it?"

"Easy, when Dalton catches up with Jake, he is going to castrate him," Amber said, turning the cart and heading for the front of the store.

Chapter Twenty-Three

"All done," Amber said, closing the book she'd been reading to Daxton.

Daxton took the book from her. "No all done."

"Yes all done. It's bedtime," Amber said firmly.

"No bedtime. Read to horsey," he said, holding up a fistful of horses.

Amber smiled. "Okay, you read horsey one book and then it's bedtime."

Appeased, Daxton took the book, slid off her lap, and carried it to his chair beside the bookshelf. He started to place the book on the chair, dropped the plastic horses, bent to retrieve the horses, and the book slid from his hand. His face took on a puzzled look as if trying to decide which items to pick up first. Finally, he dropped to the ground, picked up the horse, opened the book, and started repeating his version of the story she'd just read to him. He held on to the little grey-spotted horse, showing it the pictures as he read. While Daxton played with all the horses Dalton bought for him, the little grey horse was his favorite because Dalton had told him it was his horse and someday he would have one just like it. Amber smiled, knowing that someday was fast approaching as Dalton had everyone he knew searching for one that looked just like the appaloosa he'd chosen for his son. Finding the horse was not the issue; finding one that was suitable for a three-year-old child was another matter.

Amber pushed back in the rocker, letting her gaze drift to the large mural on the nursery wall. Her painted horse stood staring out at her with an image of Dalton's horse grazing nearby. Jake had promised to add an image of Daxton's horse, and now she wondered if that would ever happen.

She bit at her bottom lip, her attention turning back to Daxton, who looked a great deal like Julie at that age. Both Julie and Daxton took after their biological father in hair and eye coloring. Amber couldn't help wondering what Julie's child would look like. Would the baby have the same features as Julie and Daxton or would it have red hair like Jake? Most likely the latter. Her mind drifted down the hallway, wondering which of the unused bedrooms Julie would choose. Would she choose to stay in her current room and make one of the nearby guest rooms a nursery or move to another wing of the house to give her and the baby more privacy?

What if she decided to marry Jake and move out? The thought caught her by surprise. She was too young to get married; then again, she was too young to have a baby, but it was happening.

History repeating itself.

A light knock startled her. "Am I interrupting anything?"

"No, come on in, Dad," Amber replied, motioning him in.

"Grandpa, horsey is reading the book," Daxton said from his spot on the floor.

"He sure is, Buddy." Travis walked over to where Amber was sitting, looked at the matching rocker that sat empty, hesitated, sitting only when Amber nodded her approval.

"You look tired, Pumpkin," he said, once seated.

Amber gave him a once over, wondering if he'd been drinking. He looked as if he had not slept in weeks; his eyes were sunken, his cheeks hollowed. Still, he was clean, freshly shaven and he smelled of Old Spice. "You're one to speak; just look at you."

"Oh, I'm okay. And I haven't been drinking if that's what you are thinking," he said, keeping his voice lowered.

She studied him for a moment, embarrassed. "How did we get here, Dad?"

"I think Dalton brought us here."

She shook her head. "No, not here as in now. How did we get to this point? I see you, and all I can think is has he been drinking. You walk into the room and wait for permission to sit in an empty seat. How did we get here?"

Travis sighed. "Years of practice, I guess."

"I'm tired, Dad."

"I know. You have had a lot on your plate lately," he said with a nod to Daxton.

Amber felt tears forming. "No...Dad, I'm tired of this," she said, waving her hand to indicate she was talking of them.

He swallowed before speaking. "I knew my being here would be tough on you, but I was hoping

I could make it up to you. I guess I was wrong. Maybe...maybe I should leave."

The tears that threatened now flowed like a faucet, running down Amber's cheeks. "Is that what you want?"

"No, of course it is not what I want. What I want is for you to be happy."

"I am happy."

He touched her face and caught a tear. "Sure looks that way to me."

She batted her eyes to stop the flow. "I'm just so damn emotional lately."

"I think given everything that's going on in your life, you have every right to be emotional."

She laughed. "You don't even know the half of it."

"I'm afraid I do."

Amber blinked her shock. "You do? How?"

It was Travis's turn to chuckle. "Little girl, this may be a big ranch, but it is also a tight family. Not a lot goes on around here that everyone doesn't know."

"Who told you?" She knew the answer the second she saw the blush spreading across her father's cheeks. "Barbara?"

He answered with a nod. "Apparently, Julie told Maggie about the family meeting this evening, and when Maggie pried, Julie finally told her that you were insisting that she bring everyone together to tell them she is pregnant."

"Actually, the family meeting was her idea."

"That little girl is a sassy one. Barb said Maggie told her Julie looked pleased when she told her the news."

"Barb, huh?" Amber said, raising her brows. "You two seem pretty close."

He shrugged. "It's nice to have someone to talk to who doesn't judge me."

She knew that remark was aimed at her. "I remembered something a bit ago. I remembered when Mom got sick, you came to me and tried to tell me what was going on. I pushed you away. I remember you trying several times and each time I shut you out. I think maybe it's my fault."

"Don't you say that!" He looked to Daxton, who had stopped playing with his horses and was now staring at them. "It's okay, little buddy. Grandpa is just talking to Mommy."

Travis waited for Daxton to return to his book and then lowered his voice. "Don't you ever try to take this on yourself. None of what I did was your fault."

"I just keep thinking that maybe if I'd listened…"

"My name is Travis, and I'm an alcoholic. I did this on my own. I picked up that first bottle, and I took that first drink and every drink after that. I did it. Not you or anyone else. No one handed me that bottle. No one held a gun to my head and made me drink. It was my choice. Quitting is also my choice, and I am doing a pretty good job of it. Sure, I've gotten weak on occasion, but when I do, I turn to my sponsor, and we talk it through." He pulled a gold coin from his pocket and handed it to her.

Though it had been in his pocket, the coin was cool to the touch. Amber turned it in her hand, studying it. The writing around the edge was a repeated verse that read *to thine own self be true.* The center was blue with a gold triangle. Outside the triangle, the words Unity, Service, and Recovery were written in gold. Inside the triangle was a gold circle with the Roman numeral II. She looked at him. "This shows two years of sobriety. You've lived here nearly four."

Another shrug. "I'm not perfect. I fell off the wagon a couple of times and had to start over. I have a new sponsor. One that helps me see the rewards of being clean. I've been sober for two years now."

Amber felt the weight of the coin in her hand and held on to it for several moments before returning it to him. "I don't want you to leave."

He pocketed the coin. "Do you trust me?"

"I want to." It wasn't a full admission of trust, but it was all she could offer at this point.

Growing tired, Daxton returned, climbing onto her lap. Yawning, he leaned back against her and studied the little grey horse. She kissed him on the top of his head and pushed the chair into a gentle rock.

"I was in a dark place before. I am not there now," Travis said softly.

"Two years. Does that mean you are cured?"

He searched her face before speaking. "I have a disease. There is no cure. I take things one day at a time."

"But you don't want to drink anymore, do you?"

"Oh God, yes. Not a day goes by that I don't want one. But I remind myself what I want more than a drink."

"And that is?"

"I want to be a part of your life. I want to be a part of my grandkids' lives," he said with a nod to Daxton. "He's asleep, by the way."

Amber looked down at the boy, who'd grown limp in her arms.

"Let me get him," Travis said, rising. Carefully, he gathered the boy up and carried him to his wagon wheel bed. He pulled the cover over him and handed him the little black and white stuffed horse that he insisted on sleeping with each night and kissed his forehead before returning.

Amber rose as he approached.

"I remember when you used to tuck me in like that. You'd kiss me on the forehead, tell me goodnight. When I was scared or sad, you would tell me everything was going to be okay. That was long before Mom got sick and I always believed you. There were so many times afterwards that I wanted you to hug me and tell me it was all a bad dream and that everything was going to be okay. I'm tired of tiptoeing around our feelings, of being afraid to let you in. I'm afraid of being hurt again." She was crying again, her voice breaking as she spoke.

He pulled her into his arms and held her while she cried. His arms felt thinner now, but his embrace brought back so many memories. He kissed the top of her head as she sobbed, telling her over and over how sorry he was he'd let her down, assuring her that everything was going to be all right.

"I missed you, Daddy."

"I'm here now, Pumpkin," he said with a sob.

"Don't go. I don't want to lose you again."

"I'm not going anywhere," he said, hugging her once again. Amber returned his hug, both trembling, as the pain of the past seemed to slowly ebb away.

Chapter Twenty-Four

Amber stood in the spacious hallway, listening to the hum of voices coming from the family room. Spirits were high, and laughter drifted from the room in carefree ease. It sounded more like a holiday get-together than a serious declaration of unwedded improprieties.

"There you are," Dalton said, coming up behind her. "Katie Mae is up in her room playing with her tablet. She promised to keep an ear out for Daxton in case he wakes up."

She turned to face him. His hair was neatly combed and still damp from the shower. He was freshly shaved, wearing Polo Black cologne, which always drove her wild. She'd once asked him about the cologne, wondering if it was his late wife who had picked it for him. Dalton told her he'd picked it up during a quick trip to the mall. When Amber complimented him on picking the perfect cologne for him, he'd smiled then admitted he'd only picked it because there was a horse on the bottle. Amber smiled, remembering the conversation.

Dalton returned her smile, his blue eyes twinkling. "You seem to be in good spirits, considering."

"I was just thinking how good you smell and wishing this was all over and we could be alone." *Yeah, right. I'd fall asleep the second my head hit the pillow.*

Dalton's smile faded as he took in her haggard appearance. "Amber Mae, I know I'm not supposed to say this, but you don't look so good."

"That's putting it mildly," Robin said as she joined them in the hallway. "I know we did some serious power shopping today, but damn, sister, you look like shit!"

Amber forced a smile. "I'm just tired. I want this day to be over so we can start figuring out how we are going to handle this situation."

"Sounds like you are the only one worried about things to come," Robin said as the sounds of Julie's laughter drifted from the family room.

Amber sighed. "It's as if she doesn't realize the seriousness of the situation."

"She's young and in love," Dalton replied. "Is everyone here?"

"Not everyone. Jake is still missing in action. Kelly came with your sister. Tim is working late and couldn't make it on such short notice. I'm not sure how Lana feels about the situation, but Kelly and Julie have been laughing and chatting like school girls. I haven't had a chance to chat with your parents. They arrived a few moments ago. I think they are the only ones who don't know what the meeting is about."

Dalton gave a sly smile. "They know."

Robin laughed. "Best kept secrets. So, instead of a declaration of guilt, this is a celebration?"

"Oh no," Amber said, shaking her head. "I don't care if everyone already knows, Julie is still going to stand up and tell them herself. She is not going to get away with this."

"Um, given her current situation, I don't think she has gotten away with anything," Robin countered.

"What I mean is she is going to have to take responsibility for her own actions."

Robin slid a glance to Dalton. "And the boy? What is going to happen to him?"

"If he ever shows his face around here again, I will deal with him," Dalton replied.

"You know castration is illegal, right?" Robin asked, snickering.

Dalton's brows went up. "You told her?"

"She tells me everything," Robin said before Amber could reply.

Amber narrowed her eyes at her friend.

"Even the juicy stuff," Robin added, causing Dalton's face to take on a pink hue.

"Mom, are you guys ready?" Julie asked, sticking her head around the corner.

"We are waiting for Jake," Amber replied.

"Oh, he's not coming."

"Not coming?!" both Amber and Dalton said at once. "What do you mean not coming?"

"Just that," Julie said flippantly.

"Does he know what is going on tonight?" Amber asked, the anger apparent in her voice.

"He does, and that is why he's not coming. He said doing it like this is wrong, and he does not want to be a part of it."

"This is wrong?" Amber said heatedly. "He thinks this is wrong and yet he had no trouble sleeping with you."

"Where are you going?" Julie cried out when Dalton grabbed his hat from the coat tree.

Amber had to give her credit; it was the first real emotion she'd shown since all this started.

"I'm going to talk to Jake," Dalton said through gritted teeth.

Julie blocked his way. "Please don't go. He wanted to call you, and I told him not to."

"Wanted to call? He should have been man enough to come see me in person. Now step aside."

Julie didn't budge. "He wanted to, but I wouldn't let him. I told him if he said anything that I wouldn't talk to him again. Please don't be mad at Jake; none of this is his fault."

"NOT HIS FAULT? How is this not his fault?" Amber said, stepping forward.

Robin placed her hands on Julie's shoulders. "I think emotions are running a bit high here. Why don't we all calm down? None of this is good for the baby."

Dalton took a step back, obviously realizing Robin was right. Robin took the action as a surrender and herded the three of them into the living room, where they were met with silence. It was obvious that those gathered had heard everything. Dalton's parents sat on a couch along the far side of the room. Looking slightly uncomfortable, they sat holding hands in silent solidarity. Dalton's sister, Lana, sat beside them, her face unreadable. Kelly, Dalton's niece and Julie's best friend, smiled at Julie as if the two were sharing a private joke. Kelly was the spitting image of her mother, who in turn was the spitting image of her own mother. Each woman was dark-haired and thin framed with enormous breasts that always drew attention. The two older women had made peace with their abundant gifts. Kelly, on the other hand, was not as grateful. Having just turned eighteen, she was already considering breast reduction surgery.

Amber loved Kelly as much as her own daughter, but at the moment, she wanted to yell at the girl and tell her there was nothing funny about the situation.

Travis and Barbara sat next to each other in single chairs that had been rearranged to face the massive fireplace, the focal point of the room. Travis made eye contact with Amber, offering a smile of encouragement. Their talk earlier really had helped to bridge the gap between them.

Maggie sat near the window, her expression as dark as the night sky on the other side of the glass. The woman prided herself on holding the family together, and at the moment, it was apparent things were on the cusp of unraveling. She narrowed her eyes at Julie as she entered. The look was lost on the girl, who sailed into the room as if she hadn't a care in the world.

Julie moved to the fireplace and stood waiting while Amber and Dalton sat on the loveseat near to where she was standing. Robin remained at the doorway, leaning against the door frame. Amber couldn't tell if it was so she could leave if things got hairy or if she was there ready to prevent anyone else from escaping.

Dalton took Amber's hand in his as Julie reached behind the clock on the mantel and pulled out a little white wand.

"You okay, darlin'?" he whispered.

"Ready as I'll ever be," Amber said, tightening the grip on his hand.

Julie held up the little wand and smiled as if she were holding a prize. It was all Amber could do not to scream at her and demand she wipe the smirk off her face.

She still thinks this is a game.

"A couple of days ago, Mom found this little wand in my room. If you don't know what it is, it is an in-home pregnancy test. For those that haven't seen them, this is how they work. You have to pee on the wand, wait a few moments, and the wand will show you if you are pregnant. See this pink line here?" she said, pointing to the center. "Well, normally, that would mean the person is not pregnant, but if you look closer, you will see a faint pink line that goes across, which means the person is pregnant."

"She sounds like a lawyer stating a case to a jury, "Amber whispered to Dalton. "She hasn't even said the test belongs to her."

"She's obviously enjoying her moment in the sun," he whispered in return.

Julie continued to enjoy the moment as she walked around the room, showing each person the wand and pointing out the faded pink line for those who questioned its existence. When she'd finished playing to the room, she returned to her original spot in front of the fireplace. "So... after finding this, Mom became angry."

"With good reason," Maggie said, coming to Amber's defense.

Julie continued, "She yelled at me and refused to listen to my side of things. If she had... well, she didn't, and that is why I wanted you all here...to hear my side."

"Jesus, Julie, this is a family meeting, not a court hearing," Amber chided.

"Not really, Mom. You see, you are the one who is guilty. You saw the test and accused me unjustly. You didn't give me the option to state my case. You didn't give me a chance to say anything. You just yelled at me because you thought I made the same mistake you did, with me."

Amber jumped from her chair. "You were not a mistake!"

"That is not what you said."

Dalton stood next to Amber. "Julie, this is so not okay. Your mother is not on trial here."

"And I am?" Julie said pointedly.

"No...no one is. Your mother told me what she said to you. She also told me that you took her words out of context. She said that her getting pregnant was a mistake, but that you were... are the best thing that ever happened to her. She told me that from the moment I met her. She told me that if I didn't feel the same way about you that there would never be any chance for us. She loves you. I love you. You are as much of a daughter to me as Katie Mae. We will work this out together. I promise. If Jake doesn't want to step up and be a man, we will deal with that too."

Julie was listening, hanging on to Dalton's every word.

"You know your mother loves you, don't you?" Dalton asked softly.

Julie nodded her head in reply.

"Then why all of this?"

"Because I wanted to hurt her the way she hurt me."

"I didn't mean to hurt you, Julie. I didn't mean for it to come out the way it did," Amber said, tears trailing down her face.

"I know," Julie said with a sob.

Amber stepped close to her daughter. "You have to calm down. It is not good for the baby."

Julie started to sob harder. Amber reached out to her and Julie melted in a sea of tears. "I'm sorry, baby," Amber repeated.

"Me too, Momma," Julie said, the sobs coming more freely.

"You have nothing to be sorry for, baby," Amber said, stroking her hair.

"Yes, I do," Julie wailed.

"Being pregnant is not the end of the world, Julie. Yes, it will change your life, but in the end, you will end up with a child that means more to you than life itself. Just you wait and see."

Julie pushed away and stared at Amber with red-rimmed eyes. "But that's the thing, Momma. I'm not pregnant. I tried to tell you, but you wouldn't listen to me."

Amber stared at Julie in disbelief. *Not pregnant? So this was, in fact, all a game. All the theatrics were for nothing.* "Then what about the pregnancy test I found in your room? How do you explain it?"

Julie blinked at her with wide doe eyes. Her sobs reduced to involuntary spasms. "I found it in your coat pocket when I borrowed your jacket. I was mad that you had kept another secret from me. I had it in my room because I was going to confront you with it. Then when you found it, you wouldn't listen. You accused me of doing things with Jake that I've never done. I wouldn't do that. Not after everything you had to go through. Don't you see, Momma? The test is not mine; it's yours. You and Dad are going to have a baby!"

Chapter Twenty-Five

An uneasy silence sifted through the room as all present stared at them, not knowing how to react. Dalton stood beside the fireplace, holding the wand, cradling it in his palm as if it were, in fact, the child she was carrying. His face showed a mingling expression of hope, disbelief, and a hint of fear.

Lana had ushered Julie out of the room with Kelly following close behind, head held low. It was clear that Kelly had known of Julie's plan, which obviously didn't go the way either girl had expected. Amber let them go. There would be enough time to deal with Julie later. There had already been enough drama for one day. Besides, she was still in shock at learning the test was hers.

Amber took a deep breath to steady herself. How could it be hers? She stood, blinking her confusion. Julie said she had found the test in her jacket pocket. Suddenly, a memory emerged. She had taken a test the morning she left for Michigan. Dalton had come into the room as she was getting ready. Having already taken a quick peek and seeing it was negative, she hid the test. The last thing she wanted was for him to see it and get his hopes up. If she hadn't been in a rush, she would have waited long enough to see the faint line that had emerged after she'd taken that first glance. The one that showed she was in fact pregnant. Instead, she'd left in search of Daxton and had completely forgotten about the test.

Would knowing I was pregnant have changed anything?

She smiled, knowing the answer was a resounding no. Daxton had only been with them a short time, and already she loved him as if he were her own.

Robin moved into the room and was the first to break the silence. "All I can say is better you than me, girlfriend."

At that, everyone was up and offering their congratulations, lending a festive air to the room once more.

Travis was the first to approach her. There was no hesitation in his approach, just a normal father walking up and wrapping his arms around a daughter. "You have had one heck of a day, Pumpkin."

She kissed him on the cheek. "I guess it is a day for new beginnings."

"For us all," he said with a smile. He stepped back, moved aside, and waited his turn to congratulate Dalton.

Maggie was the next to step up, shaking her head as eyes swept over Amber. "I knew you weren't feeling up to par. I just figured you were worn out with stress. I must be off my game. I am usually more observant than this." She motioned over to Dalton. "He is going to have a hard time with this."

Amber felt a knot form in her stomach. "Why? He wanted a child as much as I. That's why we decided to adopt."

"Of course he did. Does," Maggie corrected. "But I've seen that look on his face before."

Amber slid a glance to Dalton, who was chatting with his parents. He saw her looking and returned her smile, but the smile didn't quite meet his eyes. Maggie was right; something was off. She'd seen it when he was holding the wand. She looked at Maggie. "He's worried."

"How could he not be? He and Mary Katherine tried for such a long time to get pregnant, and then she got sick, and there was nothing he could do. That boy is going to hover over you like he did that little orange cat."

Everyone knew the story of Lucky. Shortly after his wife passed, the cat's mother had died while giving birth. Dalton cared for that kitten right along with Katie Mae, waking in the middle of the night to feed both babies, refusing help from anyone who offered.

"What should I do?"

"For starters, you need to get some rest. You have been running yourself ragged lately and worrying about the boy doesn't help. Neither did this little fiasco," Maggie said with a wave of the arms.

Amber sighed. "I did overreact when I found the wand. Maybe I had this coming."

Maggie shook her head with a tsk. "Miss Julie had a right to be upset, but she had no right getting you all worked up like she did. I have half a mind to turn her over my knee."

If only it were that easy.

"I'm afraid she's a bit too old for that," Amber replied.

"Maybe so, but she needs to know this wasn't right."

"I'll be sure to let her know," Amber said and hugged Maggie.

Barbara stepped up as soon as Maggie stepped away. "I don't know what pleases me more, that Julie isn't pregnant or that you are. "

"I'll go with Julie not being pregnant," Amber said, the relief evident in her voice.

Barbara looked around, then leaned in close. "Travis told me that you and he had a nice talk today. It warmed my heart when I saw the two of you hug. That man loves you and wants nothing more than to have his daughter back."

Amber took a chance. "The two of you are more than friends, aren't you?"

"I care for your dad a great deal," she said, sounding embarrassed to have voiced her feelings.

Amber placed a hand on Barbara's arm. "For the record, I think he feels the same way about you."

Barbara pulled herself taller. "Did he say so?"

"Not in so many words, but I could tell by the way he said your name."

"I think I had better go see to the refreshments." She turned to go, but not before Amber saw the smile that played across the woman's face.

A warm rush washed over Amber. It really was the day for new beginnings. The shock of the last hour was wearing off, and fatigue replaced the adrenaline rush she'd been feeling. Moving to the side of the room, she sank heavily into an empty chair and closed her eyes.

True to Maggie's words, Dalton was by her side in an instant. "Are you okay?"

I'm fine, just a little tired," she said, opening her eyes.

"Maybe we should take you in to have you checked," he said nervously.

"Dalton, I promise you I'm fine. It has been a long day. I was on my feet for hours shopping for Daxton."

The look on his face told her that information did nothing to relieve his tension.

"I should have gone with you."

"You would have been bored out of your mind." *And even more worried when I broke down in the middle of the aisle*, information she decided to keep to herself. Instead, she opted to change the subject. She searched the room for Dalton's parents and saw them standing in the corner chatting with her father. Dalton's father Sheldon, an older version of the man she loved, was smiling at something Travis had said. Dalton's mother, Sharon, leaned against her husband, she too smiling at the man in front of them. In her life before Dalton, she would have envied that kind of closeness. Now she realized her relationship with Dalton was an earlier version of his parents' long and lasting love. "How did your mom and dad take the news?"

"They are worried about you after all the chaos. In truth, they were a little shocked at how the evening played out, but they seem genuinely happy for us. I'm pretty sure Mom was relieved that she was not going to be a great-grandmother just yet."

"Not as happy as I am not to be becoming a grandmother. It is so unlike Julie to have taken things so far."

"I know. I think the three of us need to sit down and have a talk."

She blew out a sigh. "But not tonight."

"Agreed."

"We hate to interrupt, but we are going to call it a night," Sharon said as she and Sheldon approached. She smiled at Amber. "You've had quite the evening. You make sure our boy takes good care of you."

"He always does," Amber replied.

"Then we raised him right," Sheldon said, clamping a hand on Dalton's shoulder. "We're going to head out. Either of you need anything, you give us a call."

"Will do, Dad," Dalton said, embracing the man.

"You picked a good woman, son." She leaned over and kissed him on the cheek and turned her attention to Amber. "Get some rest and thanks for making an old woman happy."

Amber watched them walk away hand in hand, Sharon, nearly as tall as Sheldon and Dalton's six-foot-one. Amber thought of her own five-foot-seven frame.

Our baby is going to be a giant.

"A penny for your thoughts."

"I was just thinking that our baby is going to be tall."

He laughed.

"What's so funny?"

"I'm pretty sure my dad will be shopping for basketballs tomorrow. Speaking of dads, I saw you talking to yours. I don't think I've ever seen you so relaxed around him."

"We had a long chat earlier. I cried. Travis cried. I think we are going to be all right. You don't think so?" she asked at seeing his frown.

"Of course you two are going to be okay."

"Then why the frown?"

"I'm just worried about all the stress you've been under lately. You said so before when talking to Julie. All this crying and drama can't be good for the baby."

"Don't worry, Dalton. With the breakthrough Dad and I had today, and knowing our teenage daughter is not pregnant, my stress level will be considerably less."

"Even after learning you are pregnant?"

She laughed. "Honestly, I don't think that has sunk in yet."

His eyes looked troubled. "You aren't sorry, are you?"

"That I am having a baby? Our baby," she corrected. She placed her hands on her abdomen. "I've prayed for this. I wanted to give you a son."

"We have a son. Now, I want healthy. For you and the baby," he said, placing his hands on hers.

She could feel the truth in his words and once again marveled at how lucky she was to have found a man like Dalton "It really doesn't matter to you, does it?"

"Girl, boy, twins, triplets. I will love them all the same. My only hope is that you and the baby are healthy."

Once again, she saw that flicker of fear pass across his face.

"I know you are worried and I understand why. I am tired. But I am healthy."

She watched as the lines of his face relaxed.

"Just one more thing," she said, placing her hands on her stomach, "If there are more than one in here, we are hiring a nanny."

Chapter Twenty-Six

After reaching the point of near exhaustion, Amber woke feeling tired but more at peace than she'd felt in months. She turned to see if Dalton was awake, only then realizing he had slipped out of bed unnoticed. She was still lying in bed trying to collect her thoughts when her cell phone rang. She swiped it on and answered with a groggy-sounding hello.

"Mrs. Renfro, this is John Grether. Did I wake you?"

Amber sat up in bed, fully awake. She hadn't heard from her attorney since bringing Daxton home. "No, I was…no, you didn't wake me."

"I just wanted to let you know that I have things ironed out. I filed the adoption papers and do not foresee any other obstacles in the process."

"So that's it? How long before he is legally ours?"

"Technically, he already is. You have been given full custody by the birth mother. I took the papers to her myself. I had her parents, the child's grandparents, sign a separate form just to tie up all loose ends."

"How is she, Daxton's mother?"

There was a pause. "She is fading quickly."

Amber was surprised at how sad his comment made her feel. Granted, it could be the added hormones, but somehow, she didn't believe that to be the case. While she didn't like Heather, or what the woman represented, Amber knew the woman had probably been as innocent as she when she first fell under her late husband's spell. Heather was young, and now she was dying. In a last-ditch effort of saving her son, she'd offered him to her. She would always be grateful to her for that.

"Are you sure…"

He cut her off.

"You know I am not at liberty to tell you about her condition, but I assure you her condition is not genetic. Things people do to themselves are not transferable to their offspring."

So whatever had happened was self-inflicted. She must have taken Jeff's death very hard.

She wanted to voice that aloud but decided not to press the issue. He had already said more than he should have. "Mr. Grether?"

"Yes."

"If you speak with her again, please tell her thank you for sharing her son with us. Tell her we will make sure that Daxton knows she loved him enough to do what was best for him."

"I'll make sure she knows. How is the boy doing? Any problems?"

Amber let out a sigh of relief.

"Daxton's doing great. Although I think he may be giving Maggie and Barbara an anxiety disorder. Apparently, he has been raised on junk food and will not have anything to do with their home cooking. He likes peanut butter with grape jelly and will eat cheese quesadillas as long as the inside cheese does not touch the outside of the quesadilla. He likes yogurt and has a profound fondness for toaster pastries. He will not touch veggies, but he loves most fruit, so at least we can get him to eat something healthy. Oh, and he loves French fries with ketchup," she said with a smile.

"A boy after my own heart." He chuckled. "Listen, you will probably get a surprise home visit at some point, but you've got nothing to worry about. It is a routine paperwork trail and nothing more. Not in your case anyway. No one will be asking around about your family or looking for skeletons. I have no doubt your house is more than suitable for children. Just invite them in when they show up, answer all questions honestly, and you will be all set. Oh, and one more thing,"

"Yes?"

"Congratulations on becoming a mother again."

Amber thought for a moment he was speaking of her newly discovered pregnancy, but quickly realized he was speaking about Daxton. "Thank you, Mr. Grether, for everything."

"You've got a good heart, Amber. I'm just glad you finally have the right people in your life to share it with. I'll be in touch," he said and ended the call.

Amber placed the phone beside the bed and mulled over her attorney's words. "You finally have the right people in your life to share it with." Another veiled comment by a man whose job it was to be noncommittal. Mr. Grether was the attorney that picked up all the pieces when Jeff died. If not for Mr. Grether, she would probably still be dealing with the financial havoc caused by her late husband's deceit. Now he was instrumental in getting her to raise the son that Jeff had always wanted. She couldn't help wonder what Jeff would say about that. She laughed, knowing full well what he'd say. *Over my dead body.*

A shudder went through her as if the words had been whispered from the grave.

Feeling a bit queasy, she decided to remain in bed just a bit longer. On any other day, she would have blamed it on stress, but today, she was tired. The house was quiet, and she had no doubt Dalton had given strict instructions she not be disturbed. She was not usually one to take advantage of a situation, but just for today, she was not going to feel guilty about being pampered.

* * *

She woke for the second time and looked over at the clock, surprised that it was nearly eleven. The nausea had passed, and her stomach grumbled, reminding her that not only had she missed breakfast but was also in danger of missing lunch as well. She slipped out of bed, pulled the covers up, and replaced the decorative pillows as well. She went to her closet, pulled on her favorite jeans, surprised when she had to suck in her belly to get them zipped.

Well, that didn't take long.

Any other day, she would have chided herself for gaining weight and opted to skip lunch. Today she smiled, thinking instead of the baby growing inside of her. She slipped off the jeans, tossed them on the floor, and slid the hangers across the bar in search of something a bit looser. She remembered the pants being a bit snug the last time she'd worn them. However, having taken multiple pregnancy tests, she did what she'd done with every pregnancy symptom of late: chalked it up to stress, then made a mental note to eat more salads. She thought back, trying to remember the last time she'd wore the jeans and realized with a hint of alarm it was the day she'd been thrown from the horse. That meant she'd been pregnant at the time. Her heart did a flutter.

Calm down. If there were going to be any issues, you would have known long before now. Amber took a deep breath. "Easy, girl, you are going to be as paranoid about your pregnancy as your husband if you keep this up." She laughed, realizing not only was she talking to herself, she even sounded like her husband, using the same soft tone he reserved for his broodmares. The thought evoked another laugh as she remembered their all night "horse" play at the motel when he'd met her in Michigan. He'd been in rare form, and if she didn't know better, she would have picked that day as the day she'd become pregnant. He'd been so amorous and attentive. It had started when he said she reminded him of a mare in heat. Well, if she was a broodmare, he was a wild stallion. *More like a bucking bronco,* she thought as her body grew warm with the memory of him taking her in every known position. She was pretty sure they'd even made up a few new ones along the way. She closed her eyes remembering, letting her hands explore the places the memories brought to life. She was deep in exploration, when suddenly, Dalton was really there helping. She hadn't heard him come in, but she was glad he was there. His hands felt how ready she was and he looked at her with a desire that mirrored her own need.

"I need you." She was surprised at the huskiness in her words.

Once again, she could see the fear in his eyes. "But what about..."

"The baby is fine."

He didn't seem convinced.

"Remember that night at the motel?"

Understanding replaced the doubt in his eyes. "You were already pregnant."

"And multiple times before that," she said, feeling her need deepen.

Taking her hand, he led her to the bed and brushed the pillows from the bed with one swipe. He moved slowly at first, watching her face for any sign of discomfort. She smiled, wrapping her legs around him, pulling him in deeper. Encouraged, he gave in to his need and filled her completely. They were both ready; the release they were looking for came quickly. He immediately rolled over, most likely afraid of crushing the baby with his weight.

"Not one of my best performances," he said sheepishly.

"In all fairness, I had a head start."

"Still, I hope you'll be kind when relating this to Robin."

"Robin? Oh, you are afraid I will somehow tell her the mighty stallion failed to please the broodmare."

His face took on a mischievous grin. "Technically speaking, now that you are pregnant, you are no longer a broodmare."

"No?"

"No, you are now considered a dam."

"And you?"

"Oh, I'm still a stud," he said with a wink.

No argument there. "And the baby?"

"A fetus."

"I prefer 'baby.'"

He bent down, kissing the slight swell of her stomach. "I prefer 'our baby.'"

Her heart did another flutter. "I like the sound of that."

"You know what sound I like?"

She let out a moan as he nuzzled her neck.

"Yep, that's the sound," he said, pulling her close.

Chapter Twenty-Seven

Two days had passed since Julie had announced Amber's pregnancy. Neither Amber nor Dalton had spoken to their daughter about the incident, deciding to give all parties a chance to absorb the events of the evening. The couple now waited on the back patio for Julie to join them. Daxton and Katie were happily playing nearby in the enclosed play yard, originally designed for Katie Mae. Since Katie was an only child, the area was girl-oriented, complete with a pink playhouse and plastic swings in the shape of pink horses. The play area was fully fenced with heavy black steel, only a quarter of the yard in use. When Amber had questioned Dalton about the need for such a huge play area, he told her he'd allotted enough space for future growth. He had insisted on industrial fencing in case a horse should break free and attempt to push its way into the yard while Katie was playing. As Katie grew out of play houses and swings, the yard could be converted to a basketball court, rock climbing wall or just about any other thing a child would need. Last year, they had added a small polished wood dancefloor where Katie could often be found practicing her dance moves. It was perfect at the time, however, now, much to Dalton's chagrin, Katie was in the middle of that very dancefloor showing her new little brother how to pirouette.

"Look, I'm a ballerina," Daxton shouted, placing his hands above his head while doing his best to mimic Katie.

"Remind me to reconfigure the play area," Dalton said with a sigh.

Amber snickered. "You don't think boys should be allowed to dance?"

He looked at her under the brim of his cowboy hat. "Dance, yes; pirouette, no."

"I think he's adorable."

"Girls are adorable. Boys should be grubby."

"So you are getting rid of the dance floor?"

He thought about it for a moment. "No, but I think we will add a mud bog."

"Maggie would kill you."

Another sigh. "You're right. We'll add an outdoor shower as well."

Amber laughed. "Dalton Renfro, you are such a guy. Just because little boys play ballerina does not make them...soft. I supposed you are not going to let him play with dolls either."

His look was incredulous. "Of course not."

She bit her lip and nodded toward the play yard. Wearing blue shorts, a matching t-shirt, and a black cowboy hat, Daxton was also wearing his newly purchased cowboy boots that looked extremely close to the ones Dalton wore. Sitting backwards on the pink horse, he was happily clapping his hands as Katie twirled around the dancefloor.

Following her gaze, Dalton let out his third sigh in as many minutes. "Remind me to have a talk with that boy."

Amber giggled.

The back door opened, and Julie stepped out. Clad in capris and a University of Kentucky t-shirt, she took a chair across from her parents, nervously pulling her loose hair into a ponytail. With her hair up, she looked younger than her seventeen years. Much too young to have a child of her own. Amber gave thanks for the hundredth time that her baby wasn't having a baby. When she finished fixing her hair, Julie placed her hands on her lap and looked at them expectantly.

"I'm sorry," Amber said, breaking the silence. The look of shock on her daughter's face let her know she hadn't expected this. "You were expecting me to yell?"

Julie shrugged.

"We will get to that soon, but I wanted to make sure that you knew I am prepared to take ownership of my part in this," Amber told her.

"Which is a small part," Dalton said firmly.

Julie opened her mouth as if to respond, then deciding against it, stared at her hands instead.

Amber continued keeping her voice calm and nonjudgmental. "In hindsight, how do you feel about what transpired Friday night?"

Julie picked at the skin on her fingernails speaking without looking at either of them. "I screwed up."

"Was it so important to pull the prank in front of an audience?"

Julie twisted in her chair. "I didn't think of it as a prank."

"What would you call it?" Amber asked.

"I guess I thought it would be funny."

"I didn't see anyone laughing, did you?"

"Robin laughed," Julie retorted.

"Robin laughed at her own joke. No one was laughing at what you did."

"Mom, it's over. Can't we just say I screwed up and be done with it?" Julie said, raising her voice.

Amber swallowed before speaking. "I am not yelling at you. I will not tolerate you raising your voice at me. Understand?"

"Yes," Julie said faintly.

"I didn't hear you."

"Yes," she replied firmly.

"So let's see what we can do to fix this," Amber said.

Julie looked at her like she had two heads. "What is there to fix?"

"Us. This family. The whole damn situation." Amber's voice was full of frustration.

"Oh sure, I have to keep my voice down, but you can swear."

Amber caught the barest hint of a smile from Dalton, who had agreed in advance to be there for support but to allow Amber to deal with the issue. "You are right. I'm sorry. So, to rephrase, how are we going to deal with this situation?"

"I don't understand the question."

Amber rolled her neck from side to side to relieve the tension. "Haven't we had enough games?"

"Mom, I'm serious. I don't know what you want from me. I said I screwed up. Everyone knows you are pregnant. So what is there to deal with?"

Amber took in a long breath and blew it out. "Julie, I know you were mad. You took what I said out of context and blew everything out of proportion. You know the old saying that you can't unring a bell. It's true. We can't change the past, but I'm talking about everything that led up to this. The anger. The mistrust. The fact that you thought I was lying to you. This all has to stop."

"Well, you did lie."

"How do you figure?"

"You didn't tell me about Daxton. Didn't tell him either, but I guess he wants to give you a pass on that," she said, looking at Dalton.

"Julie, I promised your mother I would stay out of this, and I will as long as you two can remain civil. But…just to be clear, what your mother and I do or do not discuss is between us. Unless it pertains to you directly, it is not any of your business."

Julie rolled her eyes. "Yeah, the kid is my brother. I'm pretty sure keeping him from me is my business."

Amber spoke up. "Remember what I said about unringing a bell? I may not have handled the situation properly, but I had my reasons. Your father hurt me. I was angry, still am. Hell…sorry. I may never get over what he put me through, and that anger almost cost me…us…the chance of having Daxton in our lives." The three of them paused to look at the boy. "But we are not talking about that now. We are talking about you going into my room, finding my pregnancy test, and using it to cause me pain. Don't you think if I'd seen the true results that I would have told you?"

Julie shrugged again.

"Well, I would have. I would have told the whole family too. But I would have done it at my own pace, in my own words, and after I shared the news with your father. Dalton," Amber added when Julie opened her mouth.

"I'm sorry." Julie put up a hand. "I know those are just words, but I don't know what else to say. I was mad when you accused me, and well, I wanted to hurt you. Then later, I guess I thought it would be fun to spring it on you in front of everyone. I didn't think that maybe you'd want to tell everyone in your own way. Please don't hate me."

"Oh, baby, I could never hate you. Don't you know you are the best thing that ever happened to me?" Amber said softly.

"So we are good?" Julie asked.

"We are, but we still have a couple of things to settle."

"Which are?"

"First, if you have a problem or question, you come to Dalton or me and discuss it like adults."

"Agreed."

"Second, stay out of my closet. There is nothing but trouble in there."

Julie sniffed and wiped at her eyes. "Deal."

Amber looked over at Dalton. "Are we done here?"

Dalton nodded his head. "I think you two ladies covered everything."

"Almost," Julie said, looking at them, then stared straight at Dalton. "You are my father. Jeff was just a sperm donor. He was never any kind of father to me."

Dalton stood, and Julie rushed to him, wrapping her arms around his neck.

"I agree with both sentiments," Amber said. Her heart melted, seeing the two embrace. It was true; Jeff had never been there for Julie, but Amber was caught off guard hearing Julie voice the opinion she herself shared. While Amber thought it on more than one occasion, she had always refrained from badmouthing Jeff in front of their daughter. She made a mental note to expound on the matter once Daxton was old enough to ask questions about his birth father. If she had her way, the boy would not grow up hating Jeff as much as she and Julie did. The last thing she wanted was for Daxton to feel the same way her daughter did at that very moment. Then again, the boy already had something Julie never did, Jeff's love. Not for the first time, she looked at Julie and wondered if things might have turned out differently if she'd been born a boy. Her glance moved to Dalton and then trailed to the kids playing just beyond earshot. If given a chance to go back and do it all over, she knew she wouldn't change a thing.

Chapter Twenty-Eight

"Dalton was telling me that a few years ago, there was some kind of mix-up with the fountain and the water flowed red," Amber said as she and Robin strolled around Triangle Park in an attempt at walking off their breakfast. "It was supposed to be pink for breast cancer awareness, and somehow it was a lovely cardinal red instead."

Robin laughed. "I bet that went over well here in Wildcat Country."

"I can't even imagine. I have never seen such a rivalry as what goes on between the University of Kentucky and the University of Louisville. Dalton's mom and dad are hardcore Wildcat fans. They even have a box in the arena. The girls love it. They have gone to nearly every game this past season."

"Must be nice," Robin said, looking towards the building that housed Rupp Arena, the official stadium of the Kentucky Wildcats basketball team. "I've always been partial to the Louisville Cardinals myself."

"We should probably keep that bit of information to ourselves. It was a huge disappointment when his family found out I don't like basketball. Seriously, it was a major sin in their eyes. Those people bleed blue."

Robin laughed. "Ooohh, you are so evil."

"I know, right. I think the only thing that saved me was Julie. That girl stole their hearts from the moment they met her. His parents have always treated her like she belonged to them. Same for Daxton. I hit the jackpot with in-laws. This time around."

"You've got that right. Speaking of Julie, how have things been with her?"

Amber knew her friend was not happy with the way Julie had handled the pregnancy news. "Julie's good. We are good," she corrected.

"And the kid?"

Amber laughed. "Daxton is doing great. I was going to bring him, but he insisted on staying to help Dalton work on the new playground."

"What's wrong with the old playground? It is adorable."

"That is exactly what's wrong with the old playground," Amber replied.

Robin turned to look at her. "Huh?"

"Katie has been showing Daxton how to be a ballerina. Dalton doesn't think his son should know what a pirouette is, much less be doing them in the backyard."

"Haha, priceless!"

"Yep, so now he has enlisted help in manning up the play area. There was a whole crew working on it when I left this morning."

"Tanks, guns, and explosions?"

"I think that is more up Jack's alley," Amber said, speaking of Robin's husband. "I'm sure this will have something to do with horses. Although I can't imagine what they are going to come up with."

"Well, make sure to get pictures."

"Always. Speaking of Jack, when is that man of yours coming home?"

"As soon as the Navy gets finished with him," Robin said, frowning. "We still have a couple of months to go on this deployment."

"I still don't know how you do it."

"The option is not to do it, and that isn't an option."

"I'm just glad you were able to move back to Kentucky."

Robin laughed.

"Like I had an option. I had to be here for my bestie. Besides, who else are you going to get to babysit the baby when you go to the basketball game with the family?"

Amber laughed.

"Are you laughing because now you don't have an excuse to miss the games or because I offered to babysit?"

"Both."

"I can babysit. I've not lost a kid yet. You okay? Not too much walking for you?" Robin asked.

Amber raised her eyes at Robin. "I'm used to running several miles a day."

"Yeah, it's probably me who is tired. Do you plan on running throughout your pregnancy?"

"I should be able to. From what I've read, I can do whatever I did before I got pregnant as long as there are no issues."

"Personally, I think you are crazy."

"For running?"

"That too. But this whole pregnancy thing. I mean you have a seventeen-year-old daughter, and now you are going to have an infant. Plus the two in between."

"I only have a seventeen-year-old daughter because I had her when I was seventeen. I'm not even thirty-five. Some women wait until they are my age to even start their families."

Robin did a full-body shudder. "Better you than me, girlfriend."

"What? You don't want another little Jack running around?"

"Bite your tongue."

The timer went off on Amber's phone. She pulled it out, hit dismiss, and looked towards the coffee shop. "I better be heading across the street. I was supposed to meet Dad a few minutes ago."

"I'm glad you two have found a common thread."

"So am I."

They walked to the edge of the sidewalk. Amber pushed the button for the talking crosswalk and snickered as the audible wait command was repeated over and over as cars passed in a steady stream in front of them.

"Good thing they tell us not to step out in front of cars," Amber quipped.

Robin made a subtle motion, telling Amber to turn around. "Maybe they are not for us."

Amber turned and saw a woman coming towards them, wearing rainbow pajama pants and pushing a stroller. She stopped when she reached the corner. Amber was about to ask the age of the baby when she realized the buggy was empty.

She turned to Robin instead. "Good point."

They waited for the voice box to tell them they could go and proceeded to cross the street. Once in front of the coffee shop, Amber peered in the window. "He's not here yet. I don't see any open parking, so he must have had to use the parking garage. If you see him on the way to your car, will you let him know I'm here?'

"Will do. Enjoy your coffee."

"Already had a cup this morning. I will have to stick to decaffeinated tea."

Robin rolled her eyes. "Pregnancy is for the birds."

"Tweet tweet," Amber said, opening the door and slipping inside. She ordered her drink and grabbed the last available table. A few moments passed before she heard her name called. She went to the counter, picked up her drink, and turned to find her table no longer empty.

Shit.

Several moments passed before another table opened up. She hurried to claim it, checked the time, her glance then drifting to the door. *Wonder what's keeping Dad? He should have arrived fifteen minutes ago.* She glanced outside; traffic was heavy but moving. *Maybe he's just having trouble finding a parking spot.* It was Friday afternoon in Lexington after all. She sat sipping her tea, scrolling through Facebook on her phone, her attention drifting towards the door each time it opened. The coffee shop was filling quickly; more than one person had eyed the empty seats at her table before turning and taking their drink elsewhere.

Come on, Dad.

Amber checked the time once more. *Five more minutes and I'm calling him.*

Three minutes later, the door pushed open, and Travis entered. Hesitating in the doorway, he scanned the room. Amber held up a finger to get his attention. Travis didn't move.

Take off your sunglasses, Dad. She extended her arm into a full wave. Only after two ladies stepped around him did Travis move from where he stood. Amber's smile faded as her father started in her direction. She'd seen that glazed look before. As if to prove her suspicions, Travis stumbled, knocking against a woman, splashing the contents of the cup she was holding all over her and the magazine she was reading. The lady jumped up, pulling at her shirt in an attempt to rid herself of the hot beverage. The shirt, a thin scrub shirt with a repeated anime print, added very little barrier between the soaked fabric and skin. She glared at Travis, her face nearly as red as her brilliantly bottled hair.

"What the hell, dude?" she said heatedly.

Amber fought back tears as Travis ignored the woman, continuing towards her without so much as an apology.

Oh God, he's drunk.

As he neared, she wondered if she'd been mistaken. He was clean-shaven, freshly showered, wearing crisp denim jeans, a freshly pressed shirt, and tie. He had even taken the time to put on cologne. Old Spice, the only cologne she could ever remember him wearing, making him extremely easy to buy for at Christmas. Before her mom passed away, she would always take Amber Christmas shopping for her dad. During their excursions, Amber insisted on buying him two things: an Old Spice gift box and a new tie – the gaudier, the better. He'd been a proud man back before her mom got sick, wearing ties to work even when the dress code at his office relaxed. He would make a big deal over her color choice, always wearing them proudly, even the year when Amber had unknowingly purchased a Hanukkah tie. At eight years old, Amber only knew it was blue, a color her dad was partial to. He had smiled and proclaimed it to be the best gift ever. It was several years later when Amber learned of the ribbing he'd taken upon wearing it to the office the following Monday morning. If not for the glazed look in his eyes and the gaunt, haunted look on his face, the man standing before her would be the man she remembered, or at least an older version of the man. The father who had never disappointed her, until he began drinking.

"Puumpkinn." The word came out in a slur.

Amber felt the stares from everyone in the building. *Why had he asked her to meet him here? To show up drunk and humiliate her?* She grabbed her cup, stood, shaking her head. "I can't believe you are drinking again."

Travis blinked as if trying to focus on what she was saying. "No, I…"

"You what? It is not even noon! And you are stumbling. You promised."

Travis reached for her and Amber stepped back, avoiding his touch. She felt like a little girl again, heartbroken. Why had she let herself believe he had changed? She placed a protective hand on her abdomen. "I can't do this again, Dad. I have the kids to think of."

As she brushed around him, a woman stepped in front of her, blocking the way. Amber recognized her as the woman her father had bumped into. Amber stopped, waiting for the woman to continue her rant.

"I think you're wrong," the woman said with a nod to Travis.

"Excuse me?"

"The man… I don't think he is drunk."

Amber closed her eyes briefly. *Could this day get any worse?* The question was quickly answered when her father grasped the table, looking at her with blank eyes before tumbling forward, sending Amber, the table, and Travis crashing to the floor.

Chapter Twenty-Nine

It took Amber a moment to realize what had happened. She was on the tile floor with Travis's full weight on top of her. Thankfully, her father's body had deflected the blow from the table. Anxious voices filled the room, one of which she recognized.

"Amber! Get him off of her. She's pregnant! Someone call an ambulance," Robin's voice commanded.

Two men in business suits lifted Travis off her as if he were weightless. Several customers hurried to move the table and chairs while the men placed Travis on the floor a few feet away. The woman with red hair hovered over him, checking his eyes, smelling his breath, and calling for someone to get orange juice.

Robin helped Amber up and guided her to an easy chair near the window. "Are you okay?"

Amber took a moment to consider. She was still shaking and sore, but as far as she could tell, she was okay. "I think so. Where did you come from? I thought you'd left."

"I was leaving the garage when I saw your dad pull in. I waved and he looked straight at me but didn't respond. I even honked the horn and nothing. I don't know…it just seemed weird. Something told me to come back and check on you. I was already on my way out, so I had to leave the garage, circle the block, come back into the garage, and find a new parking spot. To be honest, I almost said screw it. I tried to call but had no service in the garage. I thought he quit drinking."

Amber felt her lips quiver. "So did I."

"Someone call an ambulance." This time, it was the redhead doing the commanding.

"I really don't think I need an ambulance," Amber said.

"It's not for you. It's for him," the redhead said, nodding towards Travis. "Although, since you are pregnant. I think you should be checked out just to be safe."

He doesn't need an ambulance; he needs a rehab. Amber was just about to voice that opinion aloud when the redhead's words stopped her.

"I overheard your conversation. He's not drunk."

"My ass!" Robin's voice was heated.

"He's an alcoholic. I've seen him like this before," Amber protested.

"I've seen this too," the woman said. "My name is Kira Thompson. I'm a nurse. Think about it, a man drunk enough to stumble in here and then pass out would probably reek of alcohol. I would have smelled it on him when he bumped into me. At first, I thought he was just being rude. Then I realized he was having a medical emergency. My guess, most likely a diabetic episode. WHERE'S THAT ORANGE JUICE?" she called over her shoulder.

Diabetic episode? Her dad didn't have diabetes. If he did, she would know. Wouldn't she? Kira was right; her dad hadn't smelled like alcohol. He'd smelled fresh like the sea, just as the commercial from her childhood promised. He hadn't smelled like alcohol in months. That was why this hurt so much. He had promised to stay sober. He even had the coin to prove it. She'd just assumed he'd been drinking. *Why hadn't she known it for what it was? Did she expect him to fail? To disappoint her like he had so many times before.* He'd tried to tell her when she first accused him, but she hadn't listened. Worse than that, she had stepped around him as if he wasn't worth her concern. He was sick, yet she was willing to leave him here. *What if she had?* The weight of the situation punched her in the gut.

I pushed him away, again.

An employee rushed over with a large glass of orange juice and attempted to hand it to Kira. Instead, Kira plugged the end of the straw with her finger, then proceeded to dribble the contents into Travis's mouth. After several such transfers, his eyes began to flutter.

"He's starting to come around. What's his name?"

"Travis…Travis Baylock; he's my father."

Kira turned her attention back to Travis. "Mr. Baylock? Travis? Can you hear me?"

The customers that remained edged closer, cutting off Amber's view. A hushed murmur traveled through the room as they all waited for some kind of response. One of the guys, who looked to be in his late teens, held his cell phone above his head, obviously filming the events.

Amber cringed, remembering her own previous experience with the media and cell phones. The last thing she wanted was for her father to end up on the evening news. She started to get up, but her legs were like Jell-O, and she didn't trust herself to stand. Not wishing to cause another scene, she nudged Robin.

"That kid is recording this."

Robin jumped up, walked over to the guy, and snatched the phone out of his hand. "The guy is sick. Show some respect."

Amber smiled. Robin always had her back. It had been like that from the first time they'd met.

"Hey, give me my phone. This is a public place. I can record if I want to," the boy said, grabbing for the phone.

There was something about Robin that made people take her seriously. Amber wasn't sure if it was an attitude she'd been born with or the fact that she was married to a Navy man and had seen a great deal of the world, but she was a force to be reckoned with when she was mad. Retaining possession of the phone, Robin pulled herself up to her full height, all five foot three inches, and glared at the boy, daring him to move. "Calm down."

"I am calm. Just hand me my damn phone." The kid's voice was more of a plea than a demand.

"I'll give it back as soon as I delete the video." Robin held the phone just beyond the boy's reach, swiped the screen with her finger, then returned it to the boy. "You record any more of this, and I'll delete more than the video."

"Bitch," the boy said, pocketing the phone.

"Yep," Robin said with a smile.

The boy pushed past the crowd and snatched up his backpack, flipping off Robin as he left the building.

"I think I pissed him off," Robin said, returning the gesture.

"I think you embarrassed him. Thank you," Amber said.

"Anytime, girlfriend."

Amber wanted to get up to check on her dad, but if she had to admit the truth, she wasn't feeling all that well. "I can't see what's going on. Is he okay?"

"Hang on. I'll check."

Amber watched as Robin stood on tiptoes in an attempt to see over the heads of the spectators. When that didn't work, she wiggled her way between them, reappearing a few seconds later.

"He's sitting up. He still looks a bit out of it, but he is talking. Want to go over there?"

Amber knew if she told Robin she wasn't feeling well, her friend would make a fuss. "No, not yet. There are enough people standing around."

All heads turned as the sirens that had been wailing in the distance grew louder. A few seconds later, an ambulance stopped in front of the building. The doors burst open, and two paramedics hurried in pushing a gurney, a police officer following close behind. The officer went to work dispersing the crowd. Amber listened as Kira explained what happened, followed by her assessment and that she'd given Travis orange juice. She then nodded to Amber, lowering her voice so as not to be heard. They waved the officer over. He too looked at Amber before walking away and speaking into his radio.

"Wonder what that's all about," Robin said.

"Probably telling them what an awful daughter I am," Amber replied.

Robin shook her head. "That's bullshit, and you know it. I thought he was drunk too."

"I know, but I should have known better," Amber said softly.

"Why? Because his track record shows you can trust him? I know you have recently begun building a bridge with the man, but his actions of the past would have led anyone to the same conclusion," Robin replied.

"Maybe," Amber said, watching as the officer approached.

"Ma'am, I understand that gentleman is your father," he said with a nod to where a paramedic was starting an IV in Travis's right arm.

"Yes, that's right."

"I just need to get some basic information for my report. Name, age, address, phone number. They will need more info once they get him to the hospital."

Amber gave the officer the information as Travis was loaded onto the gurney.

"They will be taking him to Saint Joseph's." He glanced out the window and turned his attention back to her. "The nurse over there tells me you took a nasty fall and advised we have the paramedics check you out."

As he finished his sentence, the door opened. Two additional paramedics entered, heading in their direction.

"Oh snap," Robin said, moving aside.

"I really don't think..." Amber started to get up, and for the first time, realized her pants were soaked. She sat back in the seat, her mind swirling. *Did my water break? Am I having a miscarriage? No, please, no, not our child.* She looked at the paramedics, unable to find her words until finally, she whispered, "Help me. I think I'm losing my baby."

Chapter Thirty

Amber pushed the food around on the tray with her fork. She'd never liked hospital food and today was no exception. She'd been hooked up to the fetal heart monitor for over an hour, the baby's heartbeat thumping out in strong, rapid bursts. Amber was beyond relieved when the technician told her he'd only heard a single heartbeat. Other than bruising of both body and ego, Amber and baby had checked out fine. The baby's heartbeat was where it should be, and the monitors showed no signs of contractions. Glancing at the monitor, she sighed.

"You need to eat," Robin chided.

Amber glared at her. "I hate hospital food."

Robin snagged a carrot from the tray and popped it into her mouth. "It could use a bit of flavor, but it really isn't that bad. You should eat them; they are good for the baby. Besides, I happen to know it is rare to have them bring you lunch while you are in the ER. It took a lot of begging on my part."

Amber stuck out her tongue.

"Ingrate. You're acting like a child," Robin said, reaching for another carrot.

Amber raised her fork, jabbing it at her friend's hand. "Leave my food alone."

Robin smiled. "I take it you are still mad?"

Amber rolled her eyes.

"Okay, fine. I'm sorry I laughed. But you've got to admit it is funny."

The comment elicited another eye roll from Amber.

"Come on. You would have laughed if the shoe was on the other foot. Admit it."

Darn right I would.

Amber lowered her eyelids. "Would not."

"Liar."

Amber bit her lip to stop from smiling. Robin was right. If this had happened to her, Amber would never let her live it down. That was the problem, she was never going to live this down. How on earth would she face her family? What would Dalton say?"

"Besides, you got to hear the heartbeat early. Everything is good with the baby, and you can go home as soon as Dalton brings you some dry clothes," Robin said and burst out laughing.

"You're mean!" Amber said, throwing a carrot at her.

Robin caught the carrot, plopping it into her mouth just as a woman in scrubs stepped around the curtain. The woman had long hair that trailed down her back in various shades of browns, blondes, and grays. At first, Amber thought the woman to be long overdue for a trip to the salon to have her calico hair colored. However, as she looked closer, it was easy to see the woman was simply allowing her hair to naturally transition to gray. She went to the message board, erased the previous name, and wrote "Lorie Dorn RN" in its place. "You won't be here long, but

I'm your afternoon nurse while you are. How are y'all doing?"

"Ready to go home," Amber replied.

"Soon." The woman was stone-faced as she plucked the chart from the end of the bed, pulled reading glasses from her head, wincing as a strand of her long, transitioning hair got caught in the hinge. Dislodging the hair, she donned the glasses and skimmed the notes. "In the meantime, is there anything I can get ya?"

Amber pushed the tray away from the bed. "No, I'm good."

Nurse Lorie looked at the tray and frowned. Checking the baby monitor, her frown eased. She jotted something on the chart, returned it to the end of the bed, and glanced at Robin before turning her attention back to Amber. "When was the last time you used the bathroom?"

"About two hours ago," Robin answered for her and burst out laughing for a second time.

Amber felt the flush move over her face.

"Get out!" she hissed, pointing at the curtain.

The nurse turned towards Robin, the hint of a smile still on her lips. "If you are going to upset my patient, I will have to ask you to leave."

"I'm sorry," Robin said, fighting to regain her composure.

Nurse Lorie looked to Amber for direction.

Amber crossed her arms and let out a heavy sigh. "She can stay."

Satisfied, Nurse Lorie left, closing the curtain behind her. Suddenly, the curtain moved, and Nurse

Lorie's face appeared, the rest of her still hidden by the curtain.

Amber jumped at the sudden reappearance.

"Yes?" Robin asked, obviously every bit as startled as Amber.

"Use the buzzer if you have to use the bathroom. We have one close, so you should be able to make it." And she was gone without another word.

"Laugh, and I'll stab you with my fork!" Amber threatened.

Robin threw her hands up and turned her back, shoulders heaving.

"Sheesh, that was something out of *The Shining*," Robin said after she'd gained her composure.

"And she wasn't even there. I'll never be able to step foot in that coffee shop again."

"Sure you will; they won't even remember what you look like."

"You think so?" Amber's voice was hopeful.

"No, I'm pretty sure they screenshotted the video footage and are blasting your face all over the Internet. It's what I would have done at their age."

"You're mean." Amber pouted.

"I'm honest," Robin countered.

"Next time, lie to me."

"At least you won't have to worry about having a place to sit the next time you go. Once word gets out, no one will sit in that chair."

"I can't believe I pissed myself in the chair," Amber moaned.

"I'm pretty sure you did that when you hit the floor. We were just all too caught up in the moment to notice," Robin said, taking a serious turn. "Listen, I'm laughing now, but I came in just as Travis took the nose dive on top of you. Then the table crashed on top of the both of you, and I thought for sure you'd done some serious damage. I'm glad you and the baby are okay. And I'm glad your dad's okay too."

Travis was in a cubicle on the other side of the ER. He'd already been seen by the doctor and was being discharged within the hour.

"So am I," Amber said softly.

Footsteps sounded in the hallway, the curtain moved, and Dalton rushed into the room, face crinkled with worry. He tossed a bag onto the chair, hurried to Amber's side, scooping her into his arms. "I'm sorry I wasn't here sooner. Traffic was a nightmare."

"I'm all right. The baby is fine too," she said when Dalton looked at the fetal monitor that was noisily thumping next to her.

The lines on his face softened. "Is that the baby's heartbeat?"

Amber smiled. "It's not really how I thought we'd share the moment, but yes. The baby is fine, and the heartbeat is right where it should be."

Pushing her hair back, he kissed her forehead. "What happened?"

"Didn't Robin tell you?" Amber asked, looking at Robin.

"I told him the short version," Robin said.

"Which was?"

"I told him that Travis was ill, collapsed on top of you, and in the process made you spill your drink all over, thus the need for clean clothes. I told him you were upset, and they brought you here to have you checked out, just to be on the safe side. Now if you'll excuse me, I've had enough excitement for the day. I'm going home to get a hot bath. I'll let you tell him all the gory details, or not," she said, placing a hand on Amber's leg. "Let me know if you need anything."

After all the teasing, Robin hadn't told Dalton the real reason she was sitting in the emergency room. That she'd felt the dampness between her legs and totally lost it, thinking her water had broken.

Amber smiled at her best friend. "I will, and Robin?"

"Yes?"

"Thanks for not saying screw it."

"Anytime, girlfriend."

"What was that all about," Dalton asked after Robin left the room.

Amber told Dalton about waiting for Travis, then her reaction at seeing him. She told of his toppling on top of her, and about the nurse in the coffee shop who had most likely saved her father's life. She told of the exam the doctor had done when she first arrived at the ER and how they assured her both she and the baby were doing just fine. In the end, she only left out one little detail, thus maintaining at least a trace of self-esteem.

Chapter Thirty-One

Amber followed Daxton into the play yard and was amazed by the freshly renovated area. Standing next to the pink playhouse was a newly built mini barn structure, approximately ten feet high. It had a loft opening to allow the kids to slide down a bright green spiraling slide. Next to the barn was a pea gravel area with large metal trucks, bulldozers, and other toy construction equipment. The crew had done a good job of making the play area balanced for both children. Daxton ran over to the swings and climbed on top of a horse that bore a striking resemblance to the little plastic horse Dalton had purchased for Daxton. Once he was safely onboard, Amber gave the horse a push.

"Wee! Giddy up, horsey!" Daxton squealed as Amber gave the swing another push.

Amber stepped aside, watching as both swing and child sailed past, then retreated again. Daxton kicked his legs against the painted horse, clicking his encouragement. He held the reins in his right hand like he'd seen Dalton and others do. Eyes beaming with delight, he looked like a miniature cowboy, complete with cowboy hat and newly purchased western boots. Boots he refused to take off until bedtime, and even that was a struggle. It warmed her heart to see how quickly he and Dalton had taken to each other. Daxton had even started removing his hat on occasion and running his hand through his sandy blonde locks, the way she'd seen Dalton do time and time again. Amber had drawn the line when one morning she said something to the boy and Daxton had addressed her as "darlin'."

The backdoor to the house opened, and Travis stepped out. She waved to him, and he started in her direction.

"Again, higher," Daxton called out as the horse slowed. "Push again, Mommy."

"The boy is quite the daredevil," her father said as he opened the gate to the play yard.

Amber turned, watching Travis closely as he approached. He walked slowly, his normal easy gait hedged with a bit of a limp, giving her reason to believe he was just as sore as she after yesterday's fiasco.

"Grampa, look at me! I'm going so high," Daxton said, kicking the horse with delight.

"You sure are, little buddy. Hold on tight, or that horse will buck you off."

"No buck me off," Daxton said, shaking his head. "I ride like Daddy!"

"You sure do, Dax. You are a regular cowboy," Travis agreed.

"Good morning, Dad. We missed you at breakfast."

"Slept in. Best night's sleep I've had in years."

"Did you eat?"

Travis shook his head. "Oh lord, not you too."

Amber snickered. "Maggie and Barbara?"

"Those two were on me as soon as I came downstairs. Worrying over me and cackling like old wet hens. Forced me to sit and eat a full breakfast before they let up. Maggie giving me the what have you for not taking my medicine yesterday morning. Tell you the truth, I plumb forgot."

Amber had planned on giving him the same lecture but quickly decided against it. If Maggie had jumped on that bandwagon, she would see it through until it reached the grandstands. She gave the swing another shove and decided to go for a softer approach. "Ah, Dad, you love the attention, and you know it."

"I don't know what you are talking about," he mumbled. Stepping around her, he nodded towards the bench. "You sit, I'll push."

Amber did as he said, grateful for the reprieve. "If it makes you feel any better, Maggie and Barbara did the same to me this morning. I think Dalton put them up to it."

"Hold on tight, Dax. Grampa is going to give you a big push," Travis said, pushing the tail of the spotted horse swing Daxton was riding on. "Glad to see the boy on a real horse and not one of those frilly pink ones. Dalton did the painting, did he?"

Amber laughed. "He told me he did. Had a problem with his son riding on a pink horse."

"Can't say I blame him," Travis replied.

"I think we did a great job of giving the area a facelift. There were seven of us in here, all working to man the place up a bit."

"Carl said he and Dalton are going put in a mud bog and outdoor shower so that Miss Maggie doesn't have a fit every time the boy plays in the mud."

"I'm living with Neanderthals," Amber groaned.

"Anderals," Daxton repeated.

"The boy's quick. Better watch what you say around him," Travis said, slowing the horse.

"Grampa made you a sandbox. Want to see it?"

"Sandbox," Daxton repeated, scrambling off the painted horse.

"Come on, champ. I'll be right back," Travis said to Amber and led Daxton a few feet away, showing him the new box that had been added to the enclosed play yard.

It was to the left of the new barn and Amber hadn't noticed it until her father brought it to her attention. Clancy woofed from outside the gate. Travis walked over and let him in. The dog raced into the yard and made a beeline to Daxton, slopping him with doggy kisses.

"No kisses," Daxton said, pushing him away.

Clancy snuck in one last lick, then went to sniff the perimeter of the play yard. There was another woof and Lucky, the yellow cat, slipped through the fence just before Clancy caught up with him. The two had a love-hate relationship. Clancy loved chasing the cat, and the cat hated to be chased.

Travis crossed the distance, sitting beside Amber with a heavy sigh. "This getting old is for the birds."

"Yeah, but it beats the alternative," Amber replied.

"Yeah, I guess it does."

"There you are, you rotten dog," Amber said when Clancy finally came over to greet her. "You be nice to Lucky. He's older than you are. Where were you off to this morning?"

"Probably has a girlfriend hidden somewhere," Travis said, scratching the dog behind the ear.

"Well, if he does, there is nothing he can do about it."

Travis exhaled another sigh. "I'm sorry, fella."

Amber shook her head. "He's happy. Don't go giving him a complex."

"Coming from the person who took him to the vet to take all the joy out of his life."

"We live on a horse ranch. There are not a lot of dating opportunities here."

Travis's face turned crimson.

"Why, Travis Baylock, I do believe you are blushing. Are you making time with the ladies?"

"No, I'm not making time with anyone."

"But you are smitten. Which one is it? Maggie or Barbara?" Amber asked, already knowing the answer. Everyone had seen the way Barbara hovered over Travis. Bringing him extra helpings and making sure his favorite blackberry jam was always positioned right in front of his place at the table. Then there was their previous conversation where Travis had referred to her as Barb. No one else in the household had ever called her anything but Barbara.

"None of your beeswax. But it isn't Maggie. That woman could drive a man to drink," Travis said with a wink.

She laughed. "Just so you know, if you break her heart, Dalton will have you castrated."

"Just like you had that dog castrated?"

Amber shrugged. "It calmed him down. When did you build the sandbox?"

"Yesterday morning before I came to see you. That is why I got in trouble. I was in a hurry and wanted to get it finished before I left the ranch. There were so many guys working out there, I knew if I left it, one of them would finish it for me. I wanted it to be my gift to the boy. I had a quick bite and got started on the sandbox and forgot to eat lunch and didn't take my medicine. Where were the hens then? If one of them had said something, I would have taken it. Dammit to hell, this getting old crap bites."

"Language. Remember, little boys have big ears."

"Noted," Travis said, looking towards where Daxton sat playing in the sand.

Amber looked at Travis. "So how are you feeling, Dad? The truth this time."

He pushed back against the bench. "I'm good. The real question is how are you feeling?"

Amber smiled. "I'm just as good as you are."

"That bad, huh?" Travis chuckled.

"I feel like I've been thrown off a horse, again," she said, bumping against him with her shoulder.

Travis nodded. "I hear ya. Thanks for breaking my fall."

"Anytime," Amber said with a wave of the hand. "Seriously, that was some scary stuff. Why didn't you tell me?"

"You are a new mother to a three-year-old and are pregnant. You already have enough on your plate without worrying about me."

"My plate has room for more." *At least I hope so.*

"I did not come here to be a burden."

"No, you came here to be a part of this family. Families talk; they don't keep secrets."

Travis chuckled. "Want to try again?"

"Okay, starting today, no more secrets."

He reached out and shook her hand. "You got a deal."

"Dad."

"Yes?"

"I'm glad you weren't drunk."

He smiled a genuine smile. "Me too, Pumpkin."

Chapter Thirty-Two

"Okay, I'm in charge of the guest list. I need everyone's suggestions by the end of the day," Amber said, looking around the table. The party to celebrate Daxton's adoption was scheduled for the following month. It was supposed to be a small gathering of family, but every time she turned around, someone was adding someone else to the guest list. She'd hoped to have the list completed by dinner, but they'd fallen into a good deal on seven horses for the riding program and had to act quickly. Dalton was reluctant at first, citing it was going to be too much for Amber with Daxton joining their family and now Amber's surprise pregnancy. Amber had finally convinced him she was capable enough to handle getting the program up and running, and when she'd agreed to hire help, he relented. They'd spent the morning and most of the afternoon picking up the horses. A trip made even longer when Carl had called to tell them he'd finally located a well-bred appaloosa mare that had been trained by one of the best trainers in the area. She was mild-mannered and on the small side, making her the perfect choice for Daxton.

"I'm in charge of the entertainment," Dalton said, grinning.

Amber took a slice of meatloaf and passed the plate to Dalton. "Cheater."

All eyes turned towards Dalton, who looked mighty pleased with himself. Dalton forked out two slices of meatloaf and passed the plate to Maggie. "Hey, I can't help it if I'm lucky."

"Sounds like someone's got a story to tell," Maggie said, passing the plate to Julie.

Dalton reached for the potatoes. "Go ahead, darlin', tell them."

Amber plastered a cheesy grin and batted her eyelashes. "Oh no, honey, I wouldn't dream of ruining all your fun. You tell them."

"Land sakes, someone better tell us before Travis and I have to go take another sugar pill from all the sap the two of you are dripping," Maggie huffed.

Dalton sat down his fork. Raising both hands, he started his tale. "Amber and I had picked up the horses for the riding program."

"Me and Daxton were there too," Katie interrupted.

"Daxton and I," Amber corrected.

"And me too," Katie insisted.

"Yes, sweetie, we were all there," Amber agreed.

"Not Julie, Miss Maggie, Miss Barbara, and Grandpa," Katie corrected.

Amber blew out a sigh. "You are right, Katie. Let your dad finish."

"So we'd just left Louisville and were on the way to Bardstown to pick up the last H.O.R.S.E," he said, spelling the last word.

"Horse!" Katie shouted.

Dalton slid a glance at Daxton, who was picking the smaller beans out of a green bean and mushing them with his finger.

"Yes, but that one is a secret, remember?"

Katie placed a hand over her mouth. "Oh yeah, I forgot."

"We were heading down I65 and had a flat tire on the trailer."

"We had to stay in the truck," Katie said unhappily.

"We stay in the truck," Daxton said with an exaggerated pout that made everyone laugh.

"Anyway, I didn't want to wait for AAA, so I decided to change the tire myself."

Amber rolled her eyes.

"I saw that," Dalton said, forking out another slice of meatloaf. "May I continue?"

Amber rolled her palm at him. "By all means, please do."

"Well, it took a little longer than I thought, and some nice people stopped to help. Turns out the guy is an Elvis impersonator, and his girlfriend is a clown."

Travis laughed. "Were they dressed up? I didn't know the circus is in town."

"I bet that was a hoot," Barbara chimed in. "I just love me some Elvis."

"Must have been a sight to see," Maggie agreed.

Dalton sighed. "They weren't dressed up, nor with the circus, but I have the guy's card, and he and

PJ have agreed to be the entertainment at Daxton's adoption party."

"My birthday party," Daxton said, clapping his hands.

"Not a birthday party, silly. It's your adoption party," Katie corrected.

"Doption party," Daxton repeated.

"No. Adoption," Katie said firmly.

"No. 'Doption," Daxton repeated.

"It's okay Katie," Amber said at seeing the little girl's frustration. "So in short, this morning, Dalton agreed to schedule the entertainment. You know, to take some of the pressure off of me, and he did so without lifting a finger."

"Well, technically, I did," Dalton replied.

"Did what?"

"Lift a finger. I was changing the tire when Jack showed up. Just like my horoscope said."

Amber stopped in mid-bite. "Your horoscope told you that you would see Elvis?"

"No, it said I would get help with the problem at hand."

Amber groaned. "It meant in changing the tire."

"I already had the tire changed by that point," Dalton reminded her.

Amber shook her head. "You were supposed to help."

"I did help."

"But you didn't have to do anything. I was there too. I could have hired them." *Why am I mad? He did what he said he would do.*

Dalton rocked back in his chair. "How long did you talk to PJ?"

"What?"

"It's a simple question. How long did you talk to PJ?"

"I don't know. I didn't keep track." *Where are you going with this?*

"You talked to her just as long as I spoke with Jack, agreed?"

"Yes."

"In that time, did you learn anything about PJ?"

Shit. "No."

"Yet, I not only learned that Jack was an Elvis impersonator, I also learned that she was a clown. I know how they met and that they are getting married in a few weeks. So you see, I did do something. I booked the entertainment for the party."

Amber felt the anger lift. "Yes, you did, and that's why I love you."

Katie had been following the conversation intently. "I thought you were mad, Momma."

Amber looked around the table and felt her cheeks grow red. Before she could answer, Dalton answered for her.

"No, Little Bit, Mommy's not mad. She just has a case of the hormones."

"Whore...moans," Daxton repeated. He gave a heavy pause between the two words, changing their meaning entirely.

"What's so funny?" Katie asked when the rest of the table erupted in laughter.

"Grandpa made a silly face, and everyone was laughing," Travis said, sticking out his tongue and rolling his eyes.

Katie laughed, and everyone relaxed.

"You are a funny one, little brother," Julie said, smiling at Daxton.

Great, now I am having mood swings. Just what I need on top of everything else. Amber looked around the room to see if anyone was staring at her, only relaxing when it seemed that everyone had drifted into casual conversation. She tried to remember if she'd had mood swings this early when pregnant with Julie, but it had been too long to recall. She'd been lucky with Julie and hadn't experienced any morning sickness, making her wonder briefly if that meant the child she was carrying was a boy. *Every pregnancy is different.* Raised voices from the kids pulled her back to the present.

"Nutuh, when Mommy and Daddy adopt Daxton, he will only be my brother. Alice said so."

"Alice is a dweeb. He will still be my brother," Julie responded.

"Alice is not a dweeb; she's nine," Katie retorted as if being nine was explanation enough. "He will be Matthew Daxton Renfro, and you will still be Julie Michelle Wilson, so that means he won't be your brother anymore."

Amber looked over at Dalton. The two of them had been discussing this very thing the other day after learning that Daxton's adoption was going to be final at the end of the month. Dalton had surprised Amber when he asked if she thought her daughter would mind if he adopted her as well. Amber questioned if that were necessary, given Julie's age, as she'd be eighteen soon. Legally an adult. However, now, seeing the shadow that just crossed over her daughter's face, she reconsidered.

"Girls, no fighting at the dinner table," Dalton said, sending them each a stern look. "And Katie, nutuh is not a word."

"Uhhuh, Alice says it all the time," Katie countered.

Amber met Dalton's eyes and gave him a look she hoped he'd interpret to mean don't waste your time. Katie was at a very impressionable age, and no amount of arguing was going to overrule the wisdom of a nine-year-old.

He gave the slightest of nods and ran his hand through his hair. Beside him, Daxton emulated his father, leaving a streak of tomato paste from his food-smeared hands.

Chapter Thirty-Three

Amber and Dalton finished tucking in Daxton, kissed him goodnight, and left the room, leaving the door ajar so they could hear if he needed them. His room, Katie's old nursery, was located on the opposite side of the master bedroom. Katie's bedroom was across the hall one room down from Daxton. They walked the short way to Katie's room, entering through the open doorway.

"Time for bed, Little Bit," Dalton said as they entered.

"Alice gets to stay up until ten," Katie said.

"Alice doesn't live in our house," Dalton reminded her. "Did you brush your teeth?"

"I forgot," she said, scrambling out of bed, heading to her bathroom.

Amber sank into the purple easy chair. Bedrooms large enough to have a small sitting area was one of the many luxuries of the large house. It was a mansion by most people's standards, but Dalton still insisted it was just a place to call home. At first, she felt lost inside the massive home, but with so many people living under the roof, the house was always aflutter. Whether it be Maggie and Barbara cooking and cleaning or the kids romping through the halls, the house never felt lonely. Still, one thing bothered her. With Daxton across the hall and Katie one room down, it meant the baby's nursery would be located further away from the master bedroom than she felt comfortable with.

Dalton emerged from the bathroom with Katie riding piggyback. He galloped over to where Amber was sitting and offloaded Katie onto the chair next to her. "Give your mom a kiss goodnight."

"Good night, Mother," she said, kissing Amber on the cheek.

"Oh, it's Mother now?" Amber said, wrapping her arms around the little girl.

"It's what Alice calls her mommy," Katie said.

"Of course it is." Amber laughed. "And what does Alice call her daddy?"

"She doesn't have a daddy. She says she doesn't mind because she gets her mom all to herself, but I think sometimes she gets sad. I think sometimes Julie gets sad because she doesn't have a dad. I've heard her cry too."

Amber looked at Dalton, who seemed just as surprised by this as she. "Did you ask her why she was crying?"

"I tried. She said she was just thinking sad thoughts. That's why I thought that she might miss her dad. I know I'd be sad if I didn't have a daddy."

Dalton picked up Katie and carried her to her bed. He tucked her in and kissed her on top of her head. "You don't have to worry about me. I'm not going anywhere, Little Bit. And as for Julie, she does have a dad. She lives here with us. I'm her daddy now."

"I know. But you're not her real dad. You have a different name. Real dads have the same last name. Alice said so."

"You know, this might come as a big surprise, but Alice doesn't know everything."

Dalton pulled up the covers and switched off the light before Katie could protest. "Goodnight, Little Bit."

"Good night, Father."

"I'm beginning not to like this Alice kid," Amber said after they'd closed the door.

"That makes two of us," Dalton said, following her down the hall.

Amber stopped at Julie's door, knocked, and peeked inside. "She's in the shower. Give me a sec." Amber walked to the bathroom door and yelled for Julie to hear. "Hey, can you come to our room when you are finished?"

"Sure, almost done," came out Julie's muffled voice.

Dalton took Amber's hand the second she shut Julie's bedroom door, holding it as they walked down the long hallway. They peeked in on Daxton, saw he was sleeping, and pulled his door shut. Once inside their room, Amber kicked off her shoes, walked to the sitting room, sat on the couch, and put her feet on the footstool. Dalton sat on the opposite end of the couch and patted his lap. "Give them to me."

"Gladly," she said, swinging her swollen feet around.

"You've had a long day," he said, rubbing her feet. "You are taking tomorrow off."

"I have a party to plan."

"We have a party to plan."

"About that, sorry I was being… Ow," she said when he pushed harder.

"You were being pregnant," he said, easing his touch.

"It's been a while. I forgot about all the mood swings."

"Well, I expect that whore to moan even louder before this is over."

They both laughed.

"I can't believe he said that," Amber said with a soft moan.

"Out of the mouth of babes," Dalton replied.

"Speaking of which, what do you think about what Katie said? I know I thought Julie was too old to be adopted, but I'm beginning to think I was wrong."

Dalton's face brightened. "Do you think so?"

"Wow, way to make me feel better about being wrong. I'm beginning to think I can't even be trusted to make a good decision these days."

"You're pregnant, so we'll forgive you."

She tried to kick him, but he held tight to her feet. "Brat. Are you going to blame everything on my being pregnant?"

"Amber Mae, you are only going to be pregnant for five more months. I'd advise you to get all the sympathy you can," he said, releasing her feet.

"Speaking of the baby, I've been worried about something."

Dalton's brow furrowed. "Worried? What is it? Is the baby all right?"

"Yes, the baby is fine. You were just at my appointment with me, remember?"

"Then what is it, darlin'?"

"I just worry about where we are going to put the nursery. We can't move Daxton; he just got comfortable in his room, not to mention all the trouble the family and friends went to getting his room ready. And if we move Katie Mae, she might rebel. She's been good about Daxton, but if we push her out of her room…"

His face relaxed. "I see we are on the same wavelength. I'd pretty much reached the same conclusion about the kids' rooms. But something Katie just said gave me an idea."

"I'm listening."

"What if we do a bit of rearranging in here?"

"Ugh, do we have time? That's a lot to deal with before the baby is born."

"Calm down, darlin'. I said rearranging, not remodeling. We can take the couch and move it into the bedroom. There's plenty of room if we shift the bed over a bit. We can add a rocking chair in here for you to nurse the baby, and besides, it will only be temporary."

"How temporary?" Amber asked, warming to the idea.

"Well, Katie seems to think that since Alice is nine, she knows everything."

"So we use Katie's birthday to our advantage and offer her a grown-up room near Julie's as a birthday present. You're brilliant!" Amber said, finishing his train of thought.

He puffed up his chest, a smile spreading across his face. "One more hurdle."

"Which is?"

There was knock on the door.

"Just on the other side of that door," Dalton said with a frown.

"Come in," Amber called out.

"Mom, Dad?"

"We are in the sitting room. Come on in," Amber said.

Julie came in wearing Kentucky Wildcat pajamas, a towel wrapped around her head. "What's up?"

Amber moved closer to Dalton and motioned for Julie to take one of the chairs across from them.

"Am I in trouble?"

"No, why would you ask that?" Amber asked.

"Because this looks like trouble," Julie said, taking a seat.

"You are not in trouble, Julie. Dalton has something he wanted to ask you."

"Okay…"

Dalton took a deep breath and ran a hand through his hair as if trying to figure out where to begin. There were a couple of minutes of uncomfortable silence before he finally leaned forward, targeting his attention directly on Julie. When he spoke, it was as if they were the only two people in the room.

"A few years ago, I was lost. I walked around this house, and even though I was never actually alone, I felt lonely. I had Katie Mae, who I adored, but I had this pain in my heart that I thought would never heal. That's when I met your momma. I hate to use the cliché love at first sight, but that is exactly what it was. I knew the moment I met her that she'd been sent to heal my heart. When we talked, I knew it couldn't get any better than that. And then I met you."

Julie had drawn her feet up in the chair and was biting her nails, hanging on his every word.

"Julie, I didn't ask for your permission to marry your mother, and I regret that. Because when we married, I took something away from you."

"But I wanted you to marry my mom," Julie said tearfully.

"I know you did, little darlin'. But when I married your ma, I took something that linked the two of you together. I took away her name. And now we have Daxton, and once again, we are taking away that link you have with your brother."

Tears streamed down Julie's face. "It's okay. I understand."

"No. No, I don't think you do. You see, I don't want to take that away from you. You have been through way too much."

"But you have to adopt Daxton," Julie said on a sob. "You just have to. If you don't, he will be left out. The kids in school will make fun of him. You think they won't, but they will."

"Now now, calm down, little darlin'. I'm not explaining myself clearly enough. It is not that I don't want to adopt Daxton. It is just..." Dalton sank to one knee and took Julie's hands in his. "I did not ask you if I could marry your mother, but I'm asking you now. Julie Michelle Wilson, will you be my daughter? Not just live in my house and call me Dad. Will you take my name?"

Amber struggled to keep her sobs silent. The last thing she wanted to do was ruin this beautiful moment.

"You want to adopt me?" Julie said, her chest heaving.

"If you'll have me?" Dalton's voice was just as shaky as Julie's.

Julie jumped from the chair and flung her arms around Dalton's neck.

"I take this as a yes?" he sniffed.

"You've always been my dad, but this makes it real," she said with a sob.

Chapter Thirty- Four

"I can't get over how perfect everything turned out," Amber said as Dalton led her to the dancefloor.

"You're welcome," Dalton said as he took her into his arms.

Amber laughed. "And there he goes, taking all the credit, again."

"Did you do any of the work?"

"No, but neither did you."

Dalton kissed the top of her head as they swayed to the slow music. "Whose idea was it to call a party planner?"

She sighed. "Yours."

"You're welcome," he said once more.

Amber leaned into Dalton as they swayed to the slow music, mesmerized by the soft string of white lights that were strung from the rafters of the large arena. The building had been fully transformed, with a temporary dancefloor, tables complete with blue and white checked tablecloths, and matching balloons tied to the backs of chairs. A small temporary stage sat in the center where Jack, the Elvis impersonator, had performed earlier in the day. Much to Barbara's delight, he'd wore a white sequined jumpsuit and sounded remarkably like the man he was paying tribute to. After his performance, he'd changed and was now lending a hand to the clown, who was now his wife.

"PJ and Jack make a good team," Amber said, leading Dalton so that he could see.

"It's crazy how fate plays a hand in putting people in each other's paths," he said.

Like Jeff dying so that I could find you. A chill ran through her, causing her to shiver. Dalton rubbed her arms. "Are you cold? We can turn off some of the fans."

The fans in question were large industrial fans used to cool the structure enough to allow for indoor horse training during the hot Kentucky summers. They worked, as the current temperature outside was nearly one hundred degrees.

"Lord no, it's nearly eighty degrees in here."

"Then why the goosebumps?"

"I was just thinking of how you and I were put into each other's paths."

"It was meant to be," Dalton said, pulling her closer.

"I'm wondering about their path," he said, moving her around the floor so that she could see Travis and Barbara. The couple were standing in place on the dance floor, looking like love-struck kids. The song ended, but they didn't seem to notice, even when the next song came on with a livelier beat.

"Think I should toss a bucket of water on them?" Dalton asked, leading Amber back to her seat.

"No, let them enjoy themselves. It's been a long time since I've seen Dad that happy."

Amber sat at her table, turned sideways, placing her feet on the chair next to her. Dalton pulled up another chair, and Amber stopped him. "You don't have to babysit me. I'll be fine. Go mingle."

"Are you sure?"

"Dalton, look around. If I need anything, all I have to do is ask someone. Go."

He leaned forward and gave her a lingering kiss. "Okay, but I won't be gone long. I'm going to go check on the kids."

Amber looked around for Julie but didn't see her. Lana was heading her way, her large breasts glistening from the heat. She had two glasses in hand and rubbed the bottom of one across her bosom as she approached.

"Thought you could use a cold drink," Lana said, handing her the glass that hadn't been compromised.

Amber took the glass and studied the contents. There was an umbrella poking out of the clear liquid; two cherries rested under the crushed ice.

"Don't worry, it's water. I told them to make it pretty. Did Robin already leave?" Lana said, taking the seat next to her.

"Yes, she wanted to get home in time to Skype with Jack."

"So, how'd the doctor's appointment go?" Lana asked.

"It went well."

"And?"

"And what?"

Lana blew out a sigh. "What did the ultrasound say? Are you going to have a boy or a girl? Auntie Lana has to know what color to buy."

Amber took a sip of the water. "Auntie Lana is going to have to wait with the rest of us."

Lana stuck her bottom lip out. "You are seriously not going to find out? I thought you were kidding about that."

"No, we are not kidding."

"But why not? Don't you want to be prepared?"

"The baby is going to sleep in our room for now. So there is nothing to plan for."

"A name? How will you decide on a name?"

"We will have two picked out before the baby arrives."

"See right there, if you knew what you were having, you wouldn't have to call it 'the baby,'" Lana pressed.

Amber smiled as Daxton came running up. As he reached her, he patted her on her ever-expanding abdomen. "Mommy has a baby in her tummy."

Lana leaned in. "Is it a girl baby or a boy baby?"

His face took on a puzzled expression. "It's a baby baby."

"Do you want a brother or a sister?" Lana said, changing her question.

"I want a baby," Daxton said, then seeing Katie, he ran off in her direction.

"See? None of us cares as long as we get a baby," Amber said.

"How will you know what color blankets to get?"

"Nice try; we bought yellow."

"And the bassinet? You can't use a frilly bassinet if you have a little boy."

Amber choked on her drink. "I take it your brother did not show you a picture of the bassinet?"

"By the look on your face, I'm betting it's not your average bassinet?"

"No, your brother is having it custom made. Are you ready for this? The bassinet is a saddle."

"You're kidding, right?"

"Do I look like I'm kidding? It is on a base, and once the baby is too big for the bassinet, it can be converted to a chair."

"Nice."

Amber laughed.

"Has he picked out a horse for the baby yet?"

"No, but I'm sure it's coming. He was supposed to wait until today to show Daxton his horse, but he had him on the mare the day after we brought her home. The boy's a natural too. He takes after his father." Amber blushed. "Dalton."

Lana placed a hand on Amber's arm. "You don't have to do that."

"Do what?"

"Explain who Daxton's father is. Everyone in this building knows that boy is Dalton's son. It's why we are here, remember? Besides, he acts just like him."

"Daxton loves Dalton."

"And anyone with eyes can see Dalton loves that boy," Lana said, nodding behind Amber.

Amber turned to look. Dalton was having an in-depth discussion with the boy. When he finished, he picked up the child, who placed his head on Dalton's shoulder. Seconds later, the head popped up. Dalton lowered him to the floor, and Daxton raced off in the opposite direction. Dalton saw Amber looking and smiled. He pointed, asking if she was okay and she gave him a thumbs-up sign. She was just about to turn back to Lana when she saw Julie walking into the arena. She pointed, and Dalton raised a hand, indicating he'd take care of it.

The lights flickered, and the music stopped. Amber looked at her watch. "Almost nine; the party's over."

"Do you need any help cleaning up?"

"No, the party planner has all that covered. They will take care of the food tonight and come back for the rest in the morning."

"I think I'm going to go find my husband. You need to get some rest. You look beat," Lana said, hugging her.

Amber stayed at the table as people walked by saying their goodbyes. It didn't take long for the building to empty. Soon all that remained were those that lived on the premises. Carl and a couple of the ranch hands grabbed some leftovers and headed to the bunkhouse while the rest of the household milled around.

"We really have got to teach that boy a new dance," Dalton said as he watched Daxton and Katie do pirouettes on the now empty dance floor. He placed his hand on Amber's arm. "I think we have trouble."

"What makes you think that?" Amber said, watching Travis and Barbara approach.

"They're not making eye contact."

"I was wondering if it would be possible to have a little family meeting," Travis said when they neared.

"Now?" Dalton asked.

"If you don't mind. It won't take long."

"Okay, everyone please take a seat. Where's Maggie?"

"I'm here. I was just making sure all the food was inside where it belonged," she said, joining the rest.

Dalton took a seat beside Amber and extended a hand towards his father-in-law. "The floor is yours."

Travis looked at his shoes for a moment, then pulled himself up straight. "I do not mean to take away from the events of the day, but this here has been a day of celebration and I'm hoping what I have to say will add to that. When my wife passed, my world fell apart. I hit rock bottom and stayed there for a long time. It wasn't until the two of you got married that I was able to climb out of the bottle. A few times, it tried to pull me back in, but then I found something that I wanted more than that drink. I found a family. This family," he said with a flourish of the hands. "Then something amazing happened. I found love."

Amber looked at Travis and suddenly realized where this conversation was heading.

Barbara.

Travis took Barbara's hand and continued. "A few weeks back, I had an episode that scared the hell out of me. Something like that makes you take stock of your life. Makes you think about what is important. And I know what is important to me is family. I don't want to be alone anymore."

"You're not alone, Grandpa. You have all of us," Julie said.

"And I'm grateful for each and every one of you. But now I have something else. I have a woman who loves me and that woman is my wife," he said, lifting their hands into the air.

It was the first time Amber noticed the ring. A simple gold band on Barbara's left ring finger where none had ever sat before. Her eyes glistened with tears. Her face trembled as if waiting for the fallout of what her new husband had just said.

"You're married?" It was Dalton who'd spoke first.

"We are," Barbara confirmed.

"When?" Amber asked once the news sank in.

"Two weeks ago. We went to the courthouse," Travis said.

"Why didn't you tell anyone?" Dalton said, then looked at Maggie when both Travis and Barbara looked at Maggie.

"Wait, you knew?" Dalton sounded incredulous.

"I did." The large woman nodded her head.

"And you didn't tell?"

"They asked me not to."

"Now don't go giving Miss Maggie a hard time. The point is we are married, and we're happy.

We just need to know how the rest of you feel about it."

Dalton all but jumped from his seat, pulling them both into a hug. "Couldn't be happier for the both of you."

Amber watched as her father spoke, face drawn, eyes sunken; he looked old beyond his years. She'd thought the same thing each time she looked at him since the day he moved into her and Dalton's home. However, this evening, there was a sparkle in his eyes that she hadn't seen in years. It was the same sparkle she felt each time she saw Dalton. At that moment, she knew her father had indeed found what he'd been looking for ever since her mom got sick. He'd found a reason to keep living. She pushed herself off the hard chair, walked to her father, and kissed him on the cheek. Turning to Barbara, she did the same.

"Welcome to the family, Barb," she said, hugging the woman.

"I think I'll take the young'uns into the house and get them ready for bed," Maggie said, heading towards where Katie and Daxton were playing.

Travis and Barbara followed them, holding hands and whispering like teenagers as they walked away.

Chapter Thirty-Five

Dalton pulled Amber into his arms. "Are you okay?"

"I am."

"You sure?"

"I'm just tired. It's been a long day. I'm not sure I can handle any more surprises today." A shadow fell across the back opening. A second later, the shadow was replaced by Jake. He hesitated at seeing them, then seeing Julie, his face lit up. Amber saw the same response in her daughter when Julie realized Jake was in the building. It was the same look she'd just witnessed in her father's eyes. The same look that stared back whenever she looked in the mirror.

Julie is in love.

It surprised Amber that Jake was making an appearance; the boy had been keeping his distance lately. Dalton having spoken with him briefly, admonishing the boy for not being man enough to come to Dalton about Julie's plan. Dalton finally relented when Jake corroborated that Julie had told him she wouldn't speak to him if he did.

He had on a tight black t-shirt tucked into skinny jeans, his boots kicking up sawdust as he walked. He was sporting a neatly trimmed early beard, his tanned arms beautifully sculpted, making him appear strikingly handsome, and for the first time, Amber realized the boy had grown up.

Jake walked towards them, shoulders squared, obviously a man on a mission.

Amber looked at Dalton, who merely shrugged as if saying they'd find out soon enough.

"Dalton, Miss Amber, I apologize for interrupting, but I'd hoped to have a meeting with you."

"Julie, could you give us a minute?" Dalton said, turning to the girl.

"I'd rather her stay," Jake said, taking her hand and pulling her next to him.

"Something tells me I'm going to need this," Amber said, pulling out a chair and sitting down.

"Why don't we all sit?" Dalton said, following her lead.

Julie looked at Jake, who nodded in agreement.

Once seated, Jake looked them both directly in the eye and began. "I just wanted to say I'm sorry for what happened before."

Julie grabbed his arm. "You had nothing to do with that."

"I did. Please let me continue," he said, shaking his head.

Julie nodded and sat back in her chair.

"I'm not sure how I've behaved to lead you to the impression that I would ever do anything to dishonor your daughter, but whatever I did wrong, I apologize. I love all of you and would never do anything to jeopardize that. You have always been like a dad to me, and I never wanted to do anything to disappoint you."

"We know that now, son. Amber and I jumped to the wrong conclusion, and we are sorry for that," Dalton said.

Jake blew out a breath. "Just the same, sir. I want to thank you for adopting Julie and giving her your name. It's a good name, and she deserves it. But if I have my way, she won't have it for long. I don't want there to be any other misunderstandings, so I need to tell you what I did."

Amber felt her heart skip a beat. "What did you do, Jake?"

"I asked Julie to marry me," he said, holding Julie's hand.

"You did what!?" Dalton asked.

"She's too young," Amber whispered.

"I'll be eighteen next month. That is older than you were when you got married."

Amber swallowed the bile that threatened.

"She turned me down," Jake said before either of them could utter another word.

"No, I just told you I wanted to wait a couple of years," Julie said, smiling at him. "I promised my mother I would go to college. I hear there is a pretty good one right up the street."

Amber felt tears spring to her eyes. "Really?"

"Yes, but I also told Jake he could ask me again on my eighteenth birthday. I will say yes," she said, smiling at Jake. "But we will have a long engagement."

Jake sighed, and Julie turned her attention to her parents.

"When the time comes, I'd like to be married right here in this arena, surrounded by my family and friends. I love this farm, the horses, and most of all, I love both of you. I want the kind of love that the two of you have. But not yet. I just got my new name and I'd like to enjoy it for a while," she said, flashing a smile at Dalton.

"If you don't mind, I'd like to walk Julie to the house," Jake said, getting up.

Dalton looked at Amber, who nodded her agreement.

"Go ahead, son. So much for not getting any more surprises," Dalton said as soon as the kids were out of earshot.

"I'm not sure I'm all that surprised," Amber replied. "I've seen the way she looks at him. It is the same way I look at you."

"Do you honestly think they will wait a while?"

"For a while, but I don't think they'll wait as long as we'd like them to."

"You are taking this better than I thought you would."

"I've found happiness. Dad has too. All any parent wants is for their child to be happy."

"How can you be so sure Jake is the right guy for her?"

"Because Jake has an exemplary role model. While you are not flesh and blood, you are the only father that boy has ever known."

Dalton raised his eyebrows. "A month ago, we both wanted to castrate him."

"A month ago, we thought Julie was pregnant."

"What is going to keep that from happening now that they have professed their love?"

Amber rubbed her abdomen. "Because every time this baby cries, I'm going to hand it to Julie."

Dalton helped her up from her chair and drew her into his arms. "Darlin', you may just be the smartest woman on earth."

"Of course I am. I fell in love with you, didn't I?" she said, snuggling into her husband's embrace.

About the Author

Born in Louisville, Kentucky, Sherry eloped with a Navy man at the tender age of eighteen. She has lived in Kentucky, California, South Carolina, Michigan, Wisconsin, Virginia, Connecticut, Rhode Island, and Pennsylvania. Living in different areas and meeting new people from vastly different regions has been a unique gift she is grateful for. Sherry and her husband have three children and seven grandchildren. She is also the proud "mom" of three cats, Wally, Gracie, and Reggie.

Sherry got her start in writing by pledging to write a happy ending to a good friend who was going through some really tough times. The story surprised her by taking over and practically writing itself. What started off as a way to make her friend smile started her on a journey that would forever change her life. Sherry readily admits to hearing voices and is convinced that being married to her best friend for thirty-plus years goes a long way in helping her write happily-ever-afters.

Sherry's novels include Tears of Betrayal (the story that started it all), Somewhere in My Dreams (previously titled The Scars between Us), The King of My Heart, Surviving the Storm, book #1 of "The Storm Trilogy," Seems Like Yesterday, and That Feeling; Always Faithful -a novella, and "Whispers of the Past" - a short story – which is only available on e-book.

Sherry writes children's books under the name Sherry A. Jones.

Sherry is currently working on multiple manuscripts, including book two in the "That Feeling" series and the next two books in "The Storm Trilogy."

Sherry currently resides in Michigan's Thumb and spends most of her time writing from her home office. She greatly enjoys traveling to schools and signing events, where she shares her books and love of writing.